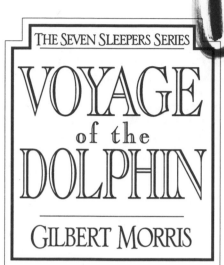

THE SEVEN SLEEPERS SERIES

VOYAGE
of the
DOLPHIN

GILBERT MORRIS

D0376883

MOODY PRESS
CHICAGO

SA PL

Moody Press, a ministry of the Moody Bible Institute,
is designed for education, evangelization, and edification.
If we may assist you in knowing more about Christ
and the Christian life, please write us without obligation:
Moody Press, c/o MLM, Chicago, Illinois 60610.

© 1996 by
GILBERT L. MORRIS

ISBN: 0-8024-3687-0

5 7 9 10 8 6

Printed in the United States of America

To Kate Larimore—
There are many fine young ladies in this world,
but you are very special to me!

If you enjoy *The Seven Sleepers,* you'll love these other great series by Gilbert Morris

- Seven Sleepers: The Lost Chronicles
- Too Smart Jones Mysteries
- The Daystar Voyages
- Bonnets and Bugles
- Dixie Morris Animal Adventures

Contents

1
Captain Daybright

The waves were slow and long and emerald green, washing up on the sandy white beach. Twenty feet out in the surf a gray rock rose like a bald head. The breakers threw white droplets over the two boys standing on it.

"Oh, come on, Reb. You're not going to get hurt. I'm surprised at you." The speaker was a small black boy wearing a red bathing suit. He was much smaller than his companion, who was tall and lanky with bleached hair and very light blue eyes. "It won't hurt you. It's just water."

Bob Lee Jackson, known as Reb to his companions, shivered and stared at Wash Jones. Then he sat down abruptly on the rock and shook his head. "Never did like water," he mumbled. "Give me some old flat Texas desert every time." He looked mournfully out at the breaking surf and said, "I'll never get used to this."

Wash grinned, his white teeth shining against his dark skin. "Shoot! I never thought I'd see the day you was more scared of something than I was."

This was true enough. The two boys were members of a group called the Seven Sleepers, teenagers who had been thrust into an alien world after the earth was ravaged by a fierce nuclear war. They had been preserved by being placed in sleep capsules programmed to keep them alive. Many years afterward, they awakened and found themselves in a world far different from even what they had seen in *Star Wars*. Much of what they had known was gone, and the planet now was inhabited not only by humans but by strange beings that sometimes seemed to come out of very bad nightmares.

Reb looked up and shook his head sadly. "Just give me a horse, and I'll be all right. But this water—it ain't natural to be swimming around in a thing like this."

"Funny thing to me," Wash said merrily, enjoying himself immensely, "you didn't mind facing a dragon back at Camelot, and now you're scared of a little old fish." He referred to the fact that Reb had almost jumped out of the water a while ago when a small fish brushed against his leg.

It delighted Wash—at fourteen, the smallest of the Sleepers—that here at last he had found at least one area in which he outdid the boldest and most active of the Seven Sleepers.

"Come on, then. Let's get off this blamed rock before an octopus or something gets us!" Reb stood to his feet, stared longingly at the shore, and then with a shout made a wild jump. He hit the water, went under, came up sputtering, and clawed his way toward the beach.

Wash made a clean dive and swam alongside.

"Come along. You can do it, Reb. Let's see you swim!"

But when they were only five feet away from land, Reb gave a terrible cry. "He got me!" he screamed. "He got me!"

"What is it?" Wash stopped swimming in alarm. He knew there *were* dangerous things in the sea, such as sharks and barracuda. He grabbed Reb's arm. "What is it? Are you hurt?"

Reb shook him off and floundered to shore, then fell on the sand and held his foot. "He got me!" he said. "I don't know what it was!"

"Let me see." Wash leaned over and grabbed the tall

boy's ankle, then said with relief, "It's OK. It's just a jelly-fish sting. You must have stepped right on it."

"It's killin' me!" Reb moaned. "I didn't know a jelly-fish had teeth!"

"They don't have teeth," Wash said, "but they've got little stinging cells, I guess. Come on, we'll put something on it."

He pulled Reb to his feet and helped him limp down the beach to where two other Sleepers were sitting on the front porch of the shack where the group was staying.

"Sarah!" Wash yelled. "You got any meat tender-izer?"

Sarah Collingwood, a small graceful girl of fifteen with brown eyes and long black hair, got up at once. She was wearing a white bathing suit that set off her tan. "What's wrong?"

"It's Reb."

"What do you want meat tenderizer for? You're not going to eat him, are you?" Josh Adams was a gangling boy with auburn hair and blue eyes. Also at fifteen, he was tall for his age. He had not filled out completely but gave evidence of being a strong man when he did. He was the leader of the Seven Sleepers.

He came off the porch and stared at Reb, who sat down, holding his foot again. "What's the matter?"

"He stepped on a jellyfish."

"Well, what are you going to do with meat tender-izer?" Reb demanded.

"Best thing in the world for a jellyfish sting or just about any other kind of sting. You got any, Sarah?"

"I don't think there is anything like that in Nuworld," Sarah said doubtfully. "Anything else work?"

"Well, some of that stuff we use for mosquito bites, I guess. That might work."

The three tried to comfort Reb, who looked very little like the courageous young man they all knew. He was bold as a lion about most things, but he hated the sea. He hated water of any kind. He also was a terrible patient.

Then two other members of the group came up. Jake Garfield was fourteen and small, with red hair and brown eyes. "What's the matter with Sir Jackson?" he said. He was jealous of Reb for his strength and made fun of him whenever he saw a weakness. "Did he stub his toe?"

The sixth member of the troop, Abbey Roberts, now joined the onlookers. She was a beautiful fourteen year old with China blue eyes and long blonde hair; and even though she wore a rather worn swimsuit, her face was carefully made up. "What's the matter, Reb?" she asked, kneeling down to look at his foot.

"I was attacked by a sea monster," Reb moaned.

"No, you weren't. You just stepped on a jellyfish." Josh laughed. "Come on, Sarah, get him some lotion."

That was the end of that adventure, but Reb did not let them forget about it. Even the next day he limped around, saying, "No, I'm not going in that water. No telling what would happen. I'd probably get bit into by a gigantic whale. That ocean ain't nothing to fool with!"

All except Wash were sitting on the front porch as Reb made this declaration yet again. They had just finished an early supper of fried fish, hush puppies, and a salad with a secret dressing that Sarah refused to identify.

It was a beautiful evening. The sun was a huge red disk in the sky, and the waves were gently lapping at the shore.

Jake leaned back, put his hands behind his head, and half closed his eyes. "This ol' beach looks like a postcard of the Gulf. I used to go down to Gulf Shores, Alabama, with my folks," he said thoughtfully. "Sure was fun." Silence fell over the group, and he added, "I'd like to do that again."

It was a familiar theme. All of them in one way or another longed for the homes that were forever gone. And all knew that they could never go home again. Still, from time to time, one of them would voice that longing, as Jake had just done.

For a while the only sound was the wind blowing through the tall sea oats and the murmuring of the ocean as it rhythmically lapped onto the shore.

Then the silence was broken as Josh sat up, saying, "There comes Wash, and he's got somebody with him."

"It's that sailor that's been taking him fishing," Sarah said. "Ryland Daybright."

Abbey sat up and began to smooth her hair back. "I declare, he's the handsomest thing," she said.

"You *would* notice that." Dave Cooper grinned. He was the oldest Sleeper and was used to Abbey's ways— she had been accustomed to admirers all of her life in Old-world and still wasn't past such things. He stared at the pair approaching and said, "They sure make a contrast, don't they? Like Mutt and Jeff."

"Who's Mutt and Jeff?" Jake demanded.

"You don't know? Characters in an old, old comic strip."

He was right about the contrast. Wash was under-sized, and Captain Ryland Daybright was well over six feet. He had blond hair that came almost down to his shoulders and a pair of cornflower blue eyes that glittered in the sun. He had a tapering face, and his skin was tanned a copper color. He looked very strong and confident. Wash had met him a month earlier and had spent most of his time since then with the captain, who was teaching him to sail, he claimed.

"Hello, Captain Daybright." Abbey smiled and got to her feet. "We've just finished eating, but there's some supper left. Sit down, and I'll get you some."

Captain Daybright flashed her a quick grin. "That might be pretty good, Miss Abbey," he said. He sat down on the porch and stretched out his long legs. He was wearing a pair of ancient white pants that were cut off above the knee and a white shirt that left his powerful arms bare. "I guess you could eat a bite, couldn't you, Wash?"

"I sure could, Cap'n." Wash grinned.

Abbey and Sarah brought out some leftover fish and hush puppies, and as they ate, Wash spoke with excitement. "Y'all ought to come on the *Dolphin*. It's the coolest boat there ever was!"

"Why'd you call it the *Dolphin*, Captain?" Josh inquired. He admired the handsome face of the captain as well as his obvious strength and agility.

"Oh, I always liked dolphins," Captain Daybright said. He washed down the last of his meal with a long drink of cool water, then held the cup in his big hands. "They stay together like family, you know. You've seen them out there, coming up out of the water with those fins of theirs. They make a pretty sight, don't they? Well, I'd like my ship to be able to sail just like that."

But even as he spoke, a frown creased Daybright's face. He shook his head and said no more.

The others talked for a while, and finally Sarah, who was always perceptive, asked, "Something wrong, Captain?"

Daybright shrugged his broad shoulders. "I guess something's always wrong, isn't it?"

His reply was so bitter that all the Sleepers turned to look at him. They had visited the ship he had been working on when they arrived at the coast and had found him to be a cheerful, optimistic young man who knew lots of songs and endless stories about the sea.

"Not like you to be so down in the mouth," Reb said. "What's the matter?"

Daybright turned the cup over in his hands. "I'm having trouble getting a crew," he said slowly.

"Why, I wouldn't think that would be hard," Wash said. "A beautiful boat like that."

"It's a *ship,* not a boat," Daybright said sharply. "If you're going to be a sailor, Wash, you've got to learn to call things by their right name." He grinned briefly at the others and said, "He called the deck a *floor* this morning. I almost pitched him over the side."

Abbey moved a little closer to the captain, her eyes fixed on his sunburned face. "I'd think that with a beautiful ship like the *Dolphin* you wouldn't have any trouble finding a crew."

"Ordinarily I wouldn't, but I've got a chance to make a voyage that most sailors would avoid." He swept the Seven with his eyes and said, "I don't guess you've ever heard of the Lost Sea?"

"I've seen it on the charts," Josh said. "Way out in the middle of nowhere."

"It's mostly uncharted waters," Captain Daybright said. "Way off the shipping lanes. All we know is a little about some of the lands that lie just on the edge of it."

"Why do you want to go there?" Dave asked. "Just for the adventure?"

"No, I've had enough adventure to last me a lifetime." Daybright smiled briefly. He set the cup down, clasped his hands together, and stared at them. "There's a man who wants to hire my ship. His name's Mennic Catalina. He's got lots of money, and he wants me to take his daughter to her wedding. Actually, he couldn't find another captain and crew willing to go."

"She's getting married to somebody out in the Lost Sea?"

"Well, there are some pretty big islands out there. The way Catalina tells it, the king of one of them has contracted to marry his daughter. The ship's captain who takes her to him will be richly paid—by Catalina and the king as well."

An irritated look crossed Abbey's face. "Why doesn't the bridegroom come for her—get married here in *her* country?"

"Can't say." Daybright shrugged. "I guess kings do pretty well what they want to."

"But what's the problem?" Dave demanded. "If her father's rich, why has he had trouble hiring a ship and crew to take her?"

"This kingdom his daughter's going to is deep in the Lost Sea. The people there are good sailors and send their ships here to the mainland often—but there are some bad currents and some seasonal winds out there. Lots of ships have started out from here for that part of the world and just never showed up again. Some say they fell off the edge of the earth." He grinned. "I know better than that, but they don't return."

"Maybe a sea monster grabbed them and pulled them down," Reb suggested. He had a vivid imagination about bad things in the ocean. "I wouldn't want to go out to a place that had things like that."

"There's nothing like that out there," Daybright said, "but there are bad winds and bad currents to drive a ship off course." His broad shoulders slumped, and his lips drew down in a frown. "This was my big chance. I've put all I could beg, borrow, or get credit for in the *Dolphin*. If I don't pay the money back right away, I'll lose her to my creditors."

"Looks like there'd be *some* sailors that would go," Josh offered. "Maybe you could promise them a bonus."

"They're all afraid of the Lost Sea—" Daybright hesitated "—and they're afraid of the ship. It's the first one I've ever built. They don't think it'll hold up in heavy seas under those winds. But I've made it better than most ships!" he said defiantly. "Put some of my own improvements in it! They say it'll break up the first time the wind blows or the waves get high."

"I'll bet it won't." Abbey smiled. "I bet it's the best ship out there."

At the age of twenty, Daybright felt a hundred years older than any of the Sleepers. But he had heard of some dramatic things they had done. He grinned at Abbey. He had known she was a flirt the first time he saw her.

Then he looked around and said longingly, "If you were all about five years older, I'd recruit you. You wouldn't be afraid to go, would you?"

"Well, I wouldn't exactly be afraid," Josh said, "but I'm pretty cautious."

"What do you mean, five years older?" Wash demanded. "I'm fourteen years old—and Dave there, he's sixteen and big as any man. We're big enough."

"Well, it's not a matter of being big or even old enough, really." Daybright smiled fondly at his small friend and slapped Wash's shoulder lightly. "You see, some people just don't do well at sea."

"That's me." Reb nodded. "I wouldn't do well at all on a long voyage. I'm not cut out for it."

"Some people aren't," Captain Daybright agreed. "You're out of sight of land. The only thing that you've got to look to is the ship that's under you and the courage of the captain and the crew."

15

"That sounds great," Wash said. He turned to the others, his eyes bright with excitement. "We've been fussing because there was nothing to do—that Goél hasn't given us any assignments for a while. Well, here's our chance. We can go on this voyage with Captain Daybright. It'll be fun."

Reb said, "No, it wouldn't be fun! We'd all probably get drowned."

"Oh, I don't think that would happen," Josh said quickly, "not with a good sailor like Captain Daybright. But we're not experienced sailors."

Daybright looked them over. They were a hearty-looking group of young people. Josh, Reb, and Dave were tall and strong. The others were healthy enough. The captain said slowly, "Well . . . ordinarily I wouldn't even think of it . . . but if you'd come with me, I'd train you, and I could pay well—as soon as the king pays me—and you'd get to see some exciting things. Sailors do get to see the world."

At once an argument broke out. Josh and Dave wanted to go. So did Sarah and Abbey. But Reb and Jake were doubtful if not downright loud in their arguments against it.

Wash, of course, was jumping up and down with excitement. "We can do it!" he cried. "We can do it! You'll just have to teach us how to raise the sails and that kind of stuff!"

Daybright nodded. "I would do that." Then he got to his feet, saying, "You talk it over. If you'd like to make a nice voyage, here's your chance. A little danger is involved—" he paused and looked around "—but I understand all of you have seen some of that. You're young, but you've lived a pretty full life, if what I hear is true."

After the captain left, the seven engaged in an argument that lasted until bedtime.

Finally Josh said, "Well, we'll all have to agree. We're here for a rest after our adventures, and maybe a sea voyage would be fun—though I think it'd be a lot of work."

"I don't mind the work," Dave said eagerly. "Just think! We could learn how to sail a ship. That could come in handy a little later. We don't know what we'll be doing for Goél."

Goél was the mysterious figure who guided their activities. He came and went without warning, often asking them to go to dangerous places.

"Well, that's just it," Wash said. "He might come at any time and ask us to go down the cone of a volcano, right into the fire. That's the kind of thing he does. Not that I mind," he said hastily, "but I think we deserve a little relaxation once in a while. I vote that we go."

Josh insisted they hold on a decision until they all were perfectly agreed.

The next morning, those in favor of the voyage began a pressure campaign, and by noon they had almost convinced Jake and Reb that a sea voyage would be a good way to spend a few weeks.

Reb was the last to give in, but finally even he threw up his hands, saying, "All right! All right! You're worse than a blasted parrot, Wash! I'll go on this old trip just to get you to hush!"

Wash let out a yell and called the others around. "Reb says he'll go! Come on, let's go tell Captain Daybright! I feel like a sailor already!"

The Seven Sleepers made their way down to the harbor, where the *Dolphin* was riding on the small swells.

Captain Daybright saw them coming and came to greet them. He met Wash's big smile with "Well, it looks like I've got me a crew. Come on aboard the *Dolphin*, then. We'll start teaching you a few things about how to sail a ship."

Reb was reluctant even to step onto the ship. He finally crawled aboard and held to the mast as if the vessel were going to drop away from under him.

"I don't like this," he said to Wash. "I'm doing it for you. So the next time I want to go on some kind of wild goose chase, you've got to pay me back."

"Yeah, sure. I'll do that," Wash said. He looked up at the mast, swaying as the ship rolled, and said happily, "This is going to be a fun time!"

2
Hoist Sails!

The *Dolphin* nuzzled into the sea, settling its prow into the foam. Then it lurched forward, and a cry went up from Abbey. She had been hauling on a rope at a command from Captain Daybright, but the sudden roll threw her off balance. Waving her arms wildly, she flew through the air, coming to land on the deck with a solid thump.

Dave, who had been pulling a rope on the starboard side, waited to see if she was hurt. Seemingly satisfied that she was not, he laughed loudly and said, "That was a neat trick, Abbey. You ought to do it again."

Getting to her feet, Abbey stared at him furiously. The fall had not hurt but had offended her sense of dignity. Rubbing her hip, she glared up balefully at the billowing sails. "I'll never learn all of this stuff!" she moaned. "It would be a lot easier if this boat had a steam engine."

"Not boat—*ship!*" Captain Daybright was standing with his feet wide apart, braced against the rolls of the vessel. He grinned at her, then came over, picked up the rope, and handed it to her. "You're doing fine, Abbey. Just give another haul now, and we'll catch a little more of this breeze."

Abbey took the rope gingerly for she had developed blisters on both hands, as had all the Sleepers. Carefully she began to pull on it and saw the white sail climb upward as she kept pace with Dave. Then there was a popping sound, the mainsail billowed out, and she felt the ship surge forward like a living thing.

Despite herself, Abbey laughed. "You know, this would be fun if it wasn't for the blisters and falling on the deck."

The *Dolphin* was out to sea on a trial run. For a week now, Daybright had been drilling the young people hard every day. They had memorized the names of the sails, the ropes that hauled them up, the spars, the ratlines, most of the parts of the ship.

It had been an exhilarating time for everybody—except Reb. Usually the most energetic and active of the Sleepers, he was one of those individuals who got seasick very easily. Once he even got seasick inside the harbor when the ship was almost as steady as the white sand on the beach.

As the *Dolphin* skimmed along over the blue-green surface of the water, Reb was standing on the spar that held the mainsail. He was not afraid of high places as a rule, but now he looked mournfully over at Wash on the other side of the spar. "I just wish this thing would stand still," he complained. "I don't care how high a tree is. I can stand that. But this here ship—it's always bobbing up and down like a cork. Or skidding sideways."

Wash knew he had an advantage over the other Sleepers. He had already been out on the *Dolphin* several times with his friend Captain Daybright. Besides, he was a born sailor, enjoying the salt spray in his face, loving to climb up to the crow's nest on the top of the mainmast. Now he looked upward and said, "Let's climb up there. We can see better, Reb."

"I can see plenty from right here!" Reb stated flatly. "You go on if you want to break your neck."

Wash laughed.

The ratlines were ropes tied in a ladder formation anchoring the mainmast to the sides of the ship. Like a squirrel, Wash stepped onto the ropes and scampered upward. When he was at the top, he popped himself into the small bucketlike structure that formed the crow's nest.

Being some thirty feet above the deck, the top of the mainmast swayed alarmingly. But Wash only grinned as the crow's nest moved from side to side and dipped forward and backward. "Better than any carnival ride I ever had," he called down to Reb. "You ought to try it."

He saw Reb merely shake his head.

Looking over the prow, covered with white-and-green foam, Wash saw the horizon hard and flat ahead. Then he heard Captain Daybright call out a command and watched Dave and Josh scurry to change the position of the sails.

"They're doing pretty good," Wash said, "for land-lubbers, that is."

He leaned back in the crow's nest, looking all around. They were out of sight of land for the first time, although he knew the shore lay only a few miles over to his left. Gazing out over the open sea, he nodded with satisfaction. "I bet we'll leave for the Lost Sea tomorrow," he said. "We can sail this old ship. It won't be any trouble for us."

Down on the fantail—the stern of the ship, which Sarah had disgraced herself by calling "the back of the boat"—Captain Daybright found Sarah and Jake sitting on the rail. "Well," he said, "what do you think you're doing? Sailors don't sit on the rail like that."

"I don't see why not." Jake popped off, shrugging his shoulders. The wind ruffled his red hair, and he ran his hand through it. "I'm just about covered with salt," he said.

"That's because the water's salty." Daybright grinned. "That's why they call sailors 'Old Salts.'" He looked at Sarah and asked, "How do you like the sea, young lady?"

Sliding off the rail, Sarah flashed him a smile. "It's fun. I'd never been on anything much larger than a row-

21

boat, but I can see how one could get caught up with ships and sailing."

"It's all I've known all my life. I was born on a ship," Daybright said.

"Where do your parents live?" Sarah inquired.

"Well, I don't have any. They got caught in a storm and went down. They had left me on shore with an uncle."

"Oh, I'm sorry," Sarah said.

"It happens at sea," Daybright said slowly. He looked out over the ocean, rolling now in longer swells that lifted the *Dolphin* up with a much slower motion. "It looks smooth right now, but I've seen it rise up like an angry beast." His expression grew hard, and he said, "The sea's got two faces. One is nice and full of sun and bright green water. The other is a beast that will smash a ship like an eggshell. I've seen waves higher than where Wash is up there on the mast, tearing everything to bits that got in their way."

Jake shifted nervously. "I hope we don't run into anything like that."

"I try to avoid it whenever possible." The captain laughed shortly, then said, "If you're the cook, Jake, you might go down and make us a little supper. I'm getting hungry."

Jake grinned. "Try to hold this thing steady. It's hard to cook when everything's banging all over the place."

"You're doing fine," Captain Daybright said affectionately. He had learned to appreciate the young redhead, who complained a lot but was always faithful.

After Jake and Sarah went below, Daybright strolled forward. He took in many things at once—the winds, their force and direction, a series of menacing-looking clouds rolling across the horizon in the east, the pitch and yaw of the ship itself. A lifetime at sea had made him aware of these things without his paying attention—things that a landsman would never notice.

Then he saw Josh and Abbey standing to one side of the forward mast, looking up at some gulls that were following the ship, their harsh cries on the air. He ambled over to them. "I guess we'll put about now. By the time we get back to shore, it'll be nearly dark."

"How do you know where we are?" Josh said, looking around. "On land you've got a tree or mountain or canyon as a marker. Here—" he waved his hand over the endless expanse of blue-green water "—it all looks alike."

"Except for the clouds," Abbey added, "and they're changing all the time."

"Well, *that* doesn't change." Daybright pointed at the setting sun, a red globe in the blue sky. "It's always the same, and at night you've got the stars. They don't change much either."

"How did you learn all this—the names of the stars and things like that, Captain?"

"Been doing it all my life. Just like you know your ABCs, I learned the names of the stars. I'll teach you more of them as we go along."

"Must be wonderful to be able to get out on the ocean and find a little pinpoint of land," Josh said wistfully. "I don't think I could ever learn how."

Daybright clapped him on the shoulder. "Sure you could, Josh. You're as bright as I was or maybe even more so. Tonight when we get in port, I'll show you some star charts. Then we'll go out and look up, and you can start memorizing the heavens."

Abbey shifted nervously then, looking at the darkening clouds on the horizon. "I don't like the looks of those," she said.

"I don't either. That's why we'd better put about."

Daybright called up to Dave, who had relieved him at the wheel. "Get ready to put about!"

"Aye, sir."

For a few moments there was activity as the sails were shifted and the ship wheeled sharply over to starboard, laying its mast alongside. Wash cried out in delight, and soon the *Dolphin* was under full sail, driven back toward the land by a following breeze.

Three hours later they pulled into the harbor.

As they nudged in and dropped anchor, Jake popped his head up from below, calling out, "Supper's ready! Come and get it before I throw it out!"

They all clambered down the ladder leading below deck to the galley where Sarah had laid out plates. Jake had fried up some steaks and added baked potatoes with them. And after Josh asked Goél's blessing, everybody plunged in. Josh noticed that even Reb, who had a queasy appetite, seemed to find himself hungry.

Daybright certainly ate with obvious enjoyment. "You're better than any cook I've had, Jake," he said. "One of them I thought we'd have to throw to the sharks."

Jake looked pleased. He said he'd always liked to cook but found it a challenge to keep the fire going in the small galley. "What do you do when a storm comes?"

"You have to douse the fire," Daybright told him. "Just one spark on this dry wood and the ship's on fire. Then you're in real trouble."

"Tell us some of the troubles you've had—adventures," Abbey said.

The Sleepers listened as the captain spoke of several dangerous times, and finally Daybright grinned. "Well, that's enough for now. Tomorrow we'll leave for the Lost Sea."

"What is the bride like?" Abbey asked, always interested in weddings and brides and romantic things like that.

Daybright shrugged. "I have no idea." He leaned back and ran his hand through his slightly curly blond hair. "I expect she's ugly as a mud fence. Her father had to sell her sight unseen to get rid of her."

"You don't mean that!" Sarah said.

Daybright laughed. "I guess not. Seems a little strange to me, though."

"It does to me too," Abbey said indignantly. "I can't imagine marrying a man I'd never even seen!"

"Well, we'll see her tomorrow," Daybright said. "They say all brides are beautiful—but I've got my doubts about this one!"

After supper they went up on deck and spent a little time tying the sails down, as they did every evening.

Suddenly a strange-looking bird appeared. Everybody looked up, and Josh asked, "What kind of a bird is that, Captain?"

Daybright stared at the bird, and Josh saw that he was troubled. "What's wrong, Captain Daybright?" he asked.

"It's an albatross." He hesitated, then shrugged, giving a half laugh. "Some sailors say it's a bird of ill omen. Bad luck."

"You don't believe that, do you?" Dave asked.

"Well, I'm not very superstitious. Not like most sailors."

However, something about the way he said the words alerted Josh. He whispered, "He really is superstitious, I think. That bird bothers him."

Everyone watched the large bird wheel, circle the ship, seem to look down at them.

"I wish he'd go away," Daybright said shortly.

"What do the sailors say?" Jake asked.

"Oh, they say when an albatross flies over a ship the day before it sails, it's a sign that the voyage will be ill-fated."

"Well, I don't believe that," Wash said defiantly. He looked around. "If I had a rock, I'd knock his head off."

"Don't do *that!*" Daybright said, his voice sharp. "I don't believe in things like that, but they say it's bad luck to kill an albatross." Then he looked at the somber faces of his youthful crew and grinned. "But all sailors are superstitious. Don't pay any attention to me. Go get a good night's sleep. We'll leave at dawn and go pick up the bride."

"It's gonna be a fun thing," Wash said, nodding emphatically as he and Reb splashed ashore. "I believe it's gonna be the funnest thing we ever did."

Reb shook his head. "I don't know about those albatrosses. The captain was sure bothered. I'd just as soon that varmint hadn't showed up."

But Wash slapped his tall friend on the back hard, saying, "Shoot, I ain't gonna let no bird spoil my vacation. We're gonna have a great time. You'll see!"

3
Here Comes the Bride

J ust as the sun rose like a huge red wafer out of the sea, the *Dolphin* put out from land. The Sleepers were busy on deck, all excited and talking about the journey. Soon the land faded into the distance, and at Daybright's command the ship swerved sharply to port.

"How long will it take us to get where we're going to get the bride?" Josh asked him.

"It's not too far. We'll be pulling in this afternoon."

They had time for a few more drills, and Daybright was pleased with his crew. As they ate a quick lunch on deck at noon, he commended them. "I've never seen land-lubbers take to the sea like you folks."

"All except Reb," Dave said, his eyes twinkling mischievously.

"Reb's doing fine," Daybright spoke up quickly. "He's not a natural sailor like Wash here, but not many people are."

Wash smiled broadly. "How 'bout if I steer the *Dolphin?*"

"Sure, you're a good helmsman." Daybright smiled. "We'll put up all the canvas we've got." He glanced around the horizon, saying, "Look at that sky! Not a cloud in it. That's the sort of thing a sailor likes to see."

"If we had an engine, we could rev it up and go three times this fast," Dave said.

"What's an 'engine'?" Daybright inquired.

Nuworld was a nontechnical place. There were no

semiautomatic weapons or airplanes or engines. The captain listened as Jake explained the ships of the old world.

"Sounds messy to me—oily and noisy," Daybright commented, looking up fondly at the white sails that billowed overhead. "The wind's good enough for me."

"What if it doesn't blow?" Abbey asked.

"Then you wait until it does. It's got to blow sooner or later."

At three o'clock that afternoon, Sarah called down to Wash, who was now at the wheel, "Land off the port bow."

They all rushed to the port side of the vessel and stared. What looked like little smudges drawn with a heavy pencil was there on the sharp horizon.

Daybright kept his position beside Wash until they got close enough to identify the land. "Put her over to port five points, Seaman."

"Aye, Captain!" Wash said. He moved the wheel, and the ship turned in the breeze with a sprightly motion.

"That's Hurricane Point. The town we're headed for is only five miles below it." Daybright looked at the small black boy and said, "I'm going to let you take us in. They'll be watching us, so do it smartly, Seaman Wash."

"Aye, aye, sir."

It took a good deal of seamanship to bring a ship into harbor. There was no motor, and the sails had to be trimmed at just the right moment. Daybright had all hands standing by, and when the moment came he cried out the command for them to strike the sails.

"You see, if I waited too long, we'd go crashing into the dock," Daybright informed Wash, whose hands were frozen to the wheel. "And if I gave it too soon, we wouldn't get in at all. We'd start drifting around out here."

"I hope we done it right, sir," Wash said anxiously.

Daybright gauged the distance to the dock. "We're all right," he said. "We'll put in right there behind that schooner."

Wash held the wheel tightly. He had had considerable practice on the open sea, but if he made a mistake now, the ship would grind into the dock and maybe do considerable damage. "I hope I don't mess up," he whispered.

But he held the ship at right angles, and Daybright had judged the speed exactly right. The *Dolphin* came to a stop not two feet away from the dock.

"Tie up!" Daybright yelled.

The Sleepers went overboard at once and tied the ropes to the wharf.

"Good job, men—and ladies." Daybright grinned. He stepped off the ship and looked around at the small harbor town. "Now we'll go find the bride," he said.

"You want me to stay here and watch the ship?"

"Some of you should, Dave. Abbey, you can stay with him if you like." He looked around, then hailed a prosperous-looking citizen, a portly man with a full beard. "Pardon me, sir, could you tell me the way to the house of Mennic Catalina?"

"That I can." The landsman turned and pointed toward the town. "Stay on that road. Mr. Catalina lives in a large house on this very street. It's across from the Boar Inn."

"I'm thanking you," Daybright said and turned to his crew. "Well, let's go get the blushing bride."

The small party made its way up from the harbor and down the main street. It was a small village with a few fine-looking houses, and the main street was lined with shops, a tavern or two, and other structures one found in a fishing village.

"There's the Boar Inn," Daybright said. He turned his head and saw a large, whitewashed building made of

29

stone. "I suppose that's Mr. Catalina's house." He marched up to the door and knocked with the brass clapper loudly.

After a few moments, the door opened, and a tall, thin individual stepped into the doorway. "What would it be for you?" he asked in a rather stilted voice.

"I am Captain Ryland Daybright, here to see Mr. Catalina."

"I'll find out if Mr. Catalina will see you."

The door closed firmly, and Daybright looked around. "Well, they didn't exactly break out a party to welcome us."

"I hope the owner's not as snooty as the butler—or whatever he is," Josh muttered.

The door finally opened again after what seemed a considerable delay. The butler wrinkled up his nose and said nasally, "You may come in." Then he looked at the young people and said, "Are these all with you, Captain Daybright?"

"Yes, the welcoming committee for the bride."

Daybright stepped past the skinny butler, and the Sleepers followed. They found themselves in a spacious foyer, and the butler said stiffly, "You may come this way, Captain—and the rest of you."

"I don't think he's impressed with us, Captain," Jake murmured, grinning. "Maybe we should have worn our tuxedos."

Wash shook his head. "He sure is snooty, ain't he now? I'd like to have him up in the crow's nest on a rough day. I bet he'd turn green as a watermelon."

The butler ushered the captain and the Sleepers into a large room with a vaulted ceiling. A glass chandelier hung down, reflecting its light on a massive, expensive-looking table surrounded by padded chairs.

At the end of the table a heavyset man with graying

hair stood at once. "My name is Mennic Catalina, and I take it this is Captain Daybright?"

"Yes, sir." Daybright studied his host. He'd never met the man. The offer to escort his daughter had come by post. "This is part of my crew, Mr. Catalina."

Catalina's full lips curled up in a smile. "Do you take your crew everywhere you go, Captain?"

"Not everywhere. But they've done a good job, and I wanted them to see the sights of the town—and to welcome the bride, of course."

"They're very young."

"Yes, they are. I like my crew to be young," Daybright said breezily. "That way they don't have any bad habits to root out." He shifted his weight and put his hands behind his back. "You'd be surprised, Mr. Catalina, what bad fellows some sailors are. Not these, though. Your daughter will be in good hands."

"Sit down, and we'll talk a little."

For the next thirty minutes Captain Daybright answered the questions that flew at him. Mr. Catalina was a sharp man and determined to get good service. Finally, after seemingly assuring himself that Daybright was capable enough from a nautical standpoint, he leaned back and said, "I'm still reluctant to trust my daughter to such a small ship."

Daybright smiled. "But I expect you had difficulty getting a larger one. Most ships don't like to go near the Lost Sea."

Catalina scowled but erased the frown immediately by passing a hand over his face. "You're a clever young fellow," he said. "That's exactly the way it was. Have you ever been in those waters?"

"Twice. Not far in, you understand, but I've touched on the islands that lie on the fringes. I can point out our course to you, if you have sea charts."

"I'll leave that to you, Captain."

Catalina fell into silence then, and Daybright understood at once that he was making a final appraisal of captain and crew. Daybright was a little nervous, for he needed this voyage badly. However, he tried to let none of this show on his face.

Finally Catalina nodded. "Very well. I know little about ships and sailing, but you have an honest face and your record is good. You're a bit young—and your crew very young—but I agree to the voyage."

Relief washed through the captain, and he said, "I'll take good care of your daughter, sir. We all will. When would you like for us to sail?"

"How's the weather? Is it good sailing weather?"

"Yes, not a cloud in the sky. No problem there. You may choose your time."

"I expect you may provision your ship tomorrow and be ready for the following day?"

"That would be fine, sir."

Catalina arose. "I'll get my daughter. Then, if it's acceptable to you, we'll walk down to the harbor with you and look over your vessel."

"At your service, Mr. Catalina."

As soon as Catalina was out of the room, Daybright wiped his brow. "That was close," he said. He grinned at the Sleepers. "I should have put false whiskers on some of you. You do look mighty young for such a voyage."

"I thought he was going to say no," Josh agreed, "but I don't think he has any choice."

"I'm anxious to see this daughter. How old is she?" Sarah asked.

"Never thought to ask. The only thing I know is, she'll probably be a spoiled brat and a lot of trouble on a voyage." He looked around at each one and warned, "If she is, I want all of you to put up with it. If you want to

32

insult somebody, come to me." He grinned then, his teeth white against his sunburned skin. "I'll throw you overboard if you do, though."

Three minutes later the door opened, and Catalina stepped inside. He waved his hand at the young woman who followed, saying, "This is my daughter, Dawn." To the girl, he said, "Dawn, this is Captain Daybright and some members of his crew."

Daybright was shocked by the beauty of the girl. For some reason he had expected a plain young woman. But now, as he looked at the beautiful creamy skin, the dark red hair, and the bright green eyes of the girl who stood there, he had to reevaluate his charge.

Blast my eyes, she's the prettiest thing I've ever seen! he thought. Aloud he said only, "Pleased to make your acquaintance, Mistress Catalina." He bowed slightly from the waist, named the members of the crew, then said, "We're honored to have your presence on the *Dolphin*."

Dawn Catalina was not smiling. Her full red lips were almost in a pout as she turned to her father. "This is the crew you expect me to sail to my wedding with?"

"Well, they're very young, my dear—"

"They certainly are." She stared straight at Wash and said, "How old are *you?*"

Wash swallowed and managed to mumble, "Almost fifteen."

"Almost fifteen? How many ships have you sailed on?"

"Well . . . actually . . . well . . . this is my first voyage."

Daybright saw trouble brewing. "They're a young crew, Mistress Dawn," he said quickly, "but as able as I've ever known a crew to be. You'll be in good hands."

The girl's eyes were an odd shade of green, he saw. They were a little like the sea itself on an early morning when the sun was shining on it. There was just a touch of blue in them. But they were sparkling with anger now, and she said huffily, "Father, have you seen the ship these . . . these . . . people came on?"

"No, my dear." Mr. Mennic Catalina seemed almost afraid of his own daughter. "That's what we were intending—to go see the vessel now."

"I'm sure you'll like the *Dolphin*," Daybright said. "If you'll allow me, we'll escort you for a tour."

For a moment he thought Dawn Catalina intended to whirl around and disappear back into her room. However, she finally sniffed and said, "Very well. I'm sure I'll find it unsuitable."

As they left the house, Josh and Sarah stayed to the rear.

"What a snob!" Josh whispered.

"She's beautiful though, isn't she?"

"Yes, she's good-looking," he agreed. He concealed a smile and said, "But I like the earthier types—like you."

Sarah turned quickly, her eyes snapping, and saw that he was grinning at her. "Oh, you—stop that!"

"I'm not kidding," Josh said. "If she goes, she's gonna be a pain in the neck. I've seen her type before."

"Where did you ever see beautiful red-haired, green-eyed princesses?"

"Ah, she's not a princess."

"Well, she's going to marry a king. That'll make her a queen. Then she can have your head chopped off."

The procession made its way down to the harbor.

The captain must be glad we policed the ship before we left, Sarah thought. Its white paint gleamed, and all the fittings were polished so that they caught the glittering sunlight.

34

"There she is, finest ship that's on the waters. I designed her myself," Daybright said.

"It's a very small boat. I want a bigger one!" Dawn Catalina insisted.

Her father cleared his throat. "Well, I'm sorry, my dear, but it seems this is the only boat available. It's not your usual voyage, you understand."

Sarah stepped forward, saying, "Miss Catalina, let me show you your quarters. I'm sure you'll like them. We've fixed them up very nicely."

Dawn stared at her and finally nodded shortly. "Very well," she sniffed.

They boarded and found Dave and Abbey waiting. Abbey stared at the bride, her eyes large, and Dave clearly appreciated the beauty of the young woman even more.

Daybright introduced these two members of the crew, then Sarah said, "Abbey, come with me. We'll show our guest her quarters."

The three young women went below.

In the cabin that had been reserved for Miss Catalina, everything was shining—there was fresh paint, a pretty blue and yellow spread on the bunk, a porthole with curtains to match. The floor was clean enough to eat on. Sarah and Abbey had polished it themselves. Everything was lovely.

But it seemed to Sarah that the girl was looking for something to criticize.

"It's so little," Dawn sneered. "My room at home is twenty times this big."

Sarah could not resist saying, "Yes, but your room at home will not get you to your fiancé."

Instantly Dawn looked at her and snapped, "I'll have none of your insolence." She seemed to expect Sarah to argue, but Sarah said nothing. "Well, I suppose it'll have to do," the bride announced, then turned and walked out.

Sarah waited until she was out the door, then shook her head, whispering to Abbey, "She *is* a pain in the neck."

"But she *is* beautiful," Abbey said.

Up on deck, the captain and Catalina waited, Daybright anxiously.

"She may decide not to go," Catalina had said when the girls went below.

Daybright recognized that this man knew his daughter well. "I'd be disappointed, sir, but that's her choice." He wanted to add, *If you had spanked her when she was smaller, you wouldn't be trembling with fear before her right now,* but this was his employer, and he could say nothing.

When the girl stepped on deck, he glanced at her face eagerly.

"It will have to do, I suppose," she said. There was a sullen pout on her lips, and she turned to Daybright. "You understand, I will expect those two girls to be my maids."

Abbey and Sarah had come on deck just in time to hear this. Both blinked in surprise, and Abbey's jaw dropped open.

At once Daybright said smoothly, "I'm sure the young ladies will do all they can to make themselves helpful. Isn't that right?"

Trapped, both nodded, and Sarah said, "We'll be happy to be of service to you, Miss Catalina."

"Very well. I will go finish packing."

"How much luggage will you have, Mistress Dawn?" Daybright inquired.

"Only eleven trunks," the girl said calmly, turned, and walked off the deck.

Mennic Catalina grinned sympathetically. "I'm sure you'll find room for my daughter's things."

"Yes, sir, of course."

"You may find her a little difficult. I'm afraid I've spoiled her."

When the men were alone again, Daybright could not help asking, "Are you satisfied with your prospective son-in-law?"

Catalina said under his breath, "Not at all, Captain." At the look of surprise on Daybright's face, he said, "This is not of my doing. From the moment my daughter heard she would be a queen, nothing would answer but that she would have this man for a husband. I hear nothing much of him except through the marriage broker, and they lie worse than lawyers."

"I see."

"I fear you are judging me harshly," Catalina said. He was silent for a moment, then added, "Well, no more harshly than I've judged myself." He turned and walked off the ship, his back stiff.

Daybright studied him as he left, then called his crew. "Let's get ready for those blasted trunks." He smiled shortly at the two girls and said, "There'll be extra pay for you for being nursemaids for Her Highness."

"You don't like her, do you, Captain?" Sarah asked.

"She's a spoiled child and needs a paddling—but they're paying us to take her to her wedding, so 'Here Comes the Bride!'"

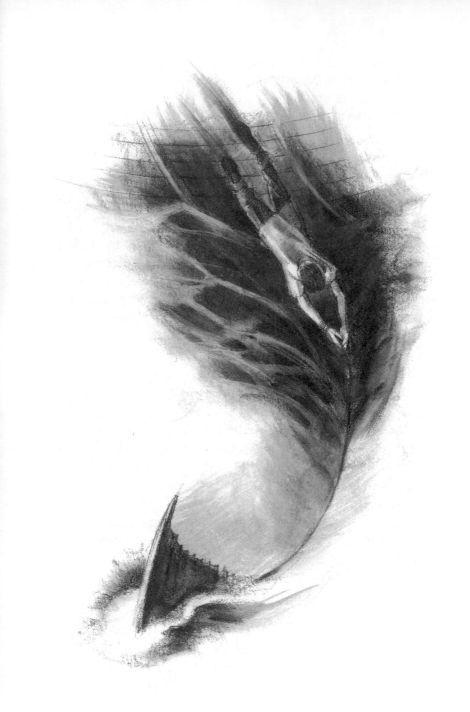

4
Cruise of the *Dolphin*

I don't care if she *is* going to be a queen. I'd like . . . I'd like to throw her overboard to the sharks!"

Sarah slammed down a plate so hard that it broke into pieces. She stared at it and with an angry motion swept it off the table.

Abbey looked a little shocked at Sarah's explosion. The older girl had always been easygoing. She seldom lost her temper, except sometimes when Josh teased her.

Stooping down, Abbey began to gather up the fragments of the plate. "Well, she is difficult, I'll admit that."

"Difficult? Nothing pleases her!"

"I guess she's used to having her own way."

"No doubt about that. She's spoiled to the bone. I don't know if I can put up with her highfalutin ways much longer."

"What's this?" Daybright stepped down into the galley where the two girls had been doing some cleaning. "Break a plate?"

"I did it," Sarah said briefly.

"Well, I break one every now and then myself." But Daybright was a quick man to see things. "Is Her Highness getting on your nerves?"

"She'd get on your nerves too, Captain, if you had to put up with her all the time. She's impossible."

Daybright said, "I know it's hard. I have the best of it—I can stay away from her, but you two have to take all of her temper tantrums."

"Nothing pleases her!" Sarah burst out. She shoved her hair back from her forehead with an angry gesture. "I thought I'd seen vile-tempered people before but nothing like her."

"I think her father's shipping her off just to get rid of her." Daybright shrugged. "She had him over the fire, I could see that."

"How much longer are we going to be on this trip?" Sarah asked suddenly. Her lips trembled with anger and humiliation. "She treats me like I was—was nothing but dirt!"

"Well, she treats everybody else the same way," Daybright said. "I had a first mate like that on my first voyage. By the time we had been out to sea for two weeks, I was ready to cut his head off."

Abbey had been moving about preparing some things for the evening meal. "You know," she said, "my guess is that she's really a nice person—underneath all that bluster."

The other two stared.

"Nice?" Sarah said. "How can you say that, the way she treats you?"

"Because I was a little like that myself when I was younger."

Daybright smiled. "Well, Granny, you're getting mighty old. How much younger were you when you were such a horrible person?"

Abbey flushed but laughed at her own words. "She's pretty and the daughter of a rich man. She's never had to make her own way. And I don't think people like that are happy."

Sarah had known, of course, that Abbey herself had been spoiled. Abbey was a beautiful girl; and as long as they had been together, Sarah had been slightly jealous of the younger girl's attractiveness.

"Something happened to me on our last adventure," Abbey said. "I learned that beauty isn't everything."

"What do you mean, Abbey?" the captain asked.

"You must have noticed that the most attractive people aren't always completely happy." Abbey spoke this with some surprise as if she thought everybody knew it. "I knew several beauty queens back in the old world."

"What's a beauty queen?" Daybright asked.

"Oh, they have contests to pick the prettiest girls," Abbey answered.

"And did they pick you?"

Abbey blushed and shrugged her shoulders. "Once or twice," she said. "I was never Miss America, but I knew some girls that went up pretty high. And you know what?" She stopped and looked at them curiously. "Those were always the ones who seemed the most insecure."

"I'd think if they were all that pretty, they wouldn't have to be insecure."

"I guess they're never satisfied. Like some men who never get enough money. Once a girl starts running on her beauty, she's always thinking about losing it—or whether the next girl is going to be prettier."

Abbey picked up a cup and wiped it slowly, her eyes thoughtful. "You never know whether someone likes you because of what you are on the outside—because you're pretty—or whether they like you for what you are."

Sarah was staring at her friend, understanding. "I've seen a little of that. I guess that's why those beautiful actors and actresses never stay married. They're always jumping from one man or one woman to the next."

"I don't understand any of this," Daybright said. "All I know is she's a royal pain in the neck."

"Yes, she is," Abbey said slowly, "and I guess she always will be—unless something happens to change her."

41

"Let her husband change her. He can take a stick to her," he joked. "That would make her see things a little differently."

Both girls laughed.

"I can see you don't know much about marriage, Captain," Sarah said. "Would you take a paddle to your bride?"

Daybright grinned. "Why, of course I would. Don't you have to treat a wife just like a horse that needs discipline?"

"Don't ever tell that to a woman you're interested in," Abbey said, sobering up. "It'd be the worst thing you could do."

"Well, I admit I don't know anything about women. All I know is ships and the ocean, and that's all I'll probably ever know."

That afternoon Wash baited a line with a small fish and threw it over the stern. He let out the line and held it for a while.

Soon Reb came back to sit beside him. "Let me hold that thing! I'm a pretty good fisherman myself."

"All right." Wash handed him the line and watched as Reb wrapped two or three turns around his wrist. "I wouldn't do that if I was you."

"Why not?"

"'Cause you might get something too big on there. Might pull you out of the boat."

"Ship." Then Reb shook his head. "Just let something get on there! I'll show you who gets pulled."

His boastful words were to haunt him; for not five minutes later, Wash, who was lolling alongside the rail, heard Reb give a cry. He turned to see the lanky Texan go sailing over the rail.

"Man overboard!" Wash yelled.

Daybright, who was at the helm, spun the wheel furiously.

All the crew members who were on deck rushed to the rail.

Dave yelled, "What was he doing?"

"He had his wrist tied onto a fish line, and something yanked him over the side. Could be a shark!"

The *Dolphin* wheeled slowly.

As the boat came alongside, it appeared Reb had managed to free himself from the fishing line. He grabbed the rope Dave threw to him and soon was standing on deck, dripping and staring at his wrist. "Look at that!" he said.

They all crowded around. His wrist was rope-burned.

"What was that you caught?"

"Nothing," Reb said, abashed. "He caught *me*." But a light of battle appeared in the boy's blue eyes. He loved a challenge and said, "You wait—I'll get that varmint."

Reb began preparing another line, but this time he looped it around a capstan, saying, "Come on, fish. You bite one more time, and we'll see what's what!"

Daybright steered the *Dolphin* back on course, and Reb stayed at the rail with the loose end of the line in his hand.

Perhaps a half an hour later Reb let out a yell, and Wash ran to see that the line was tight. Something was pulling and plunging on the end of it.

"He's a big'un, whatever he is," Reb shouted, "but I'll get him."

It turned out to be quite a battle. For more than two hours Reb struggled to bring the fish in. If it had not been for the turn taken around the capstan, he would never have been able to land it.

Daybright came to watch the struggle. "You'll never get him on board," he predicted. "He's too big."

"I'll do it or die!" Reb said and threw his head back and gave a loud Rebel yell.

Finally the fish was brought to the surface.

"It's a big marlin. It might go five hundred pounds," Daybright said. "Good eating if we can get him on board."

"Gotta be some way to do it."

"We can winch him on if I can get another hook through his mouth."

At once Daybright began throwing out lines, attaching them to a winch that was used to ease the *Dolphin* backward in a port. Then he brought a piece of iron with a hooked shape on one end. "Let me get this in him, and I think we can do it."

Apparently Dawn Catalina had heard the yelling, and she came up on deck. She was wearing a delicate pink dress made of very fine silk. It was adorned with ribbons, and she looked beautiful. But it was not a dress for the deck of a ship—especially not when landing a fish.

Daybright got the fish gaffed and then ran back and turned the winch. "Give me a hand, Dave."

The two of them worked it hard, and the huge fish came slowly over the stern.

Reb was yelling all the time, and the others were cheering enthusiastically. The boat shifted, the fish gave a sudden flip and was on deck.

"Look out," Daybright yelled. "He could stab you with that sword of his."

The fish turned sideways. He slid along the deck and gave a tremendous lunge, doubling over and releasing his tail. The tip of it caught Dawn in the stomach.

"*Oooph!*"

If the full force of the tail had caught the girl, she would have been knocked overboard. As it was, she flipped backward, legs flying and ruffled pantaloons showing in the bright sunlight.

Daybright jumped to her side, reached down, and lifted her to a sitting position. These fish were dangerous! "Are you all right, Miss Catalina?" he asked with concern.

Dawn's face was red, and she was trying to get her breath. Finally she did and began to scream incoherently. "You clumsy oaf!"

Daybright stared at her. "I'm afraid I wasn't the clumsy one," he snapped. He pulled her to her feet and looked at the slimy trail the fish's tail had made on the front of her dress.

She looked down and saw it and said, "My best dress!" She jerked away from him. "I might have expected it from you!" She flounced off and disappeared down the ladder, screaming, "Sarah! You come at once and help me clean up this awful mess!"

As soon as she was below, everyone on deck broke into wild laughter.

The fish was still flopping around, and Daybright picked up a short club and knocked him on the head. Then he looked at Sarah and said, "There'll be a bonus in this for you if you can calm her down."

Sarah grinned suddenly. "Let me borrow that club, Captain. I think I know how to handle this."

A round of laughter went up again, and Josh warned, "Don't give it to her, Captain. She'd use it. I know her!"

Sarah erased the laughter from her face and went below. The next thirty minutes were as hard as anything she'd ever had to endure. She helped Dawn remove the dress and put on fresh clothing, all the time suffering a string of insults. Nothing she did pleased the girl.

Finally she escaped and went back on deck.

Daybright was waiting. "Was it bad?"

"Bad enough." Sarah's lips were tight. She had kept her temper but only by a small margin. "You may have to use that club, Captain. I've never seen anyone so unreasonable. It was her fault, not yours or anybody else's."

"I don't think Miss Dawn Catalina is used to accepting blame for her actions." Then he added thoughtfully, his eyes turning moody, "She may have to learn that the hard way. On a long voyage, people sometimes have to face up to what they are."

At supper that night, the entire crew gathered around the table—Daybright had showed them how to tie the wheel in position to keep the ship on course.

"For a short time," he said, "we won't get too lost. Time to have a little celebration."

Jake, with some help from the others, had prepared a fine meal. None of them except Daybright had eaten marlin before, and it turned out to be a delicious fish.

Dawn came in wearing a light green dress that perfectly matched her eyes.

"That dress must have cost enough to feed a starving village for a year," Jake whispered. "Boy, she's a looker, ain't she now?"

Dawn was seated as was customary at one end of the table while Captain Daybright took the other end. The Sleepers arranged themselves, and Sarah and Reb had volunteered to serve.

"Well, now, this is fine, isn't it?" Daybright commented. "You wouldn't eat a better meal than this, Miss Catalina, in the finest castles in the land."

Dawn tasted the fish and nodded reluctantly. "It does very well. I've had better, though."

It appeared that Daybright had to grit his teeth, but he managed to smile. "And this fresh bread—I don't see how you do it, Jake. It's delicious!"

"An old family recipe," Jake said. "I grew up on it."

He grinned, his homely face bright. "That's why I'm so pretty. I ate lots of it. It's guaranteed!"

The meal was very pleasant. Dawn said nothing complimentary about the food, but everyone else did.

Finally Dawn said, "I want some more of this juice."

She held out her goblet in a demanding fashion.

Sarah arose at once and took it. She went over to where a pitcher was fastened down and filled the goblet, then started back to the table. Unfortunately, the ship shifted at that moment, causing Sarah to stumble. She caught her balance, but a few drops of the liquid fell on the bosom of Dawn's dress.

At once Dawn rose up, crying, "You clumsy girl! Can't you do anything right?" Her hand flew through the air, and she slapped Sarah on the face.

The sound of the slap was very loud and caught everybody off guard. A mutter went up from Josh, and he began rising to his feet, his face pale with anger.

Captain Daybright caught his arm in a steely grasp and forced him back down. He looked down the table and said, "It's not my custom to give lessons in manners."

A silence fell over the room.

Daybright's blue eyes were fixed on the face of the young woman, who glared back at him. "I'll have to ask you to apologize to Miss Sarah," he said quietly.

Dawn's eyes flashed with anger. Her lips curled up in a twist of arrogance. "Apologize to a servant? Never!"

Again silence fell over the room. Every one of the Sleepers turned his eyes to Daybright.

The captain leaned forward, put his hands flat on the table, and pressed them down. He'd kept his temper under firm control thus far, and he did so now. His voice was low. "I'll give you a simple choice, Miss Catalina. You'll either apologize right now—or you will have the rest of your meals in your cabin."

"You wouldn't dare!"

Daybright stared at the girl's face. It was flushed, and her lips were open in an "O" of surprise. He suspected she had never been crossed in her whole life, and he knew he was risking part of his fee to cross her now. He had been paid a portion in advance by the girl's father, the remainder to be collected from the king when she was safely delivered. But he was angry clear through, and he said firmly, "The choice is yours—apologize or go to your cabin."

"I won't be treated like this! You can't make me go to my cabin!"

"Don't force me to do something we may both regret."

Dawn's face went pale. Her lips drew into a tight, stubborn line as she shook her head. "I won't apologize, and you can't make me."

Captain Ryland Daybright rose from the table.

Dawn's eyes opened wider, and she stared at him as he moved around the table, walking with precise steps.

When he stood over her, he said, "Your last chance, Miss Catalina."

"No! You won't dare—"

Daybright pulled out her chair with one hand, grasped her arm with the other. She was a strong young woman, but the bulk of the sailor made her seem almost like a child.

"Let me go!" she cried out. She tried to slap him, but he grabbed her other hand.

He held both wrists with one hand and said, "I will take you to your cabin."

He dragged her out of the galley, and when they got to the ladder she cried, "I won't go up there! You can't make me!"

"Oh, yes, I think that can be arranged."

The Sleepers all watched as he picked her up and threw her over his shoulder. Her legs were kicking, and she was beating him on the back ineffectually with her fists, screaming with all her might.

"Put me down! Put me down!"

The captain's legs disappeared up the ladder, and his tread could be heard on the deck.

"Well, I guess we know what kind of a man our captain is," Dave said in awe. "I didn't think he'd do it."

"Well, I did," Josh said, "and he did it just right."

"You think he'll make her stay in that cabin?" Abbey asked.

"I expect he will." Wash was grinning from ear to ear. "And a good thing too. That young lady, she needs to learn how to behave herself."

Josh sidled up to where Captain Daybright was standing at the wheel, staring out to the horizon. "Getting dark, Captain," he said.

Daybright didn't answer for a moment. He was eyeing the sky. "Yes, it is. Josh, be sure things are tied down pretty well. I think we're in for a blow."

Josh looked over and saw the dark clouds on the horizon. "Why, that's a long way off."

"I know, but this air's got a blow in it. Feel the ship lifting? See those sails?"

Josh was no sailor, but he could sense something like a moody quality in the sky, and he looked anxiously at Daybright. "You think we're in for a storm?"

"I wouldn't be surprised if we had a little blow."

Josh stood there for a while before saying, "Captain, are you ever going to let Miss Catalina out of her cabin?"

"I'm not keeping her there. She can come out any time she's ready to apologize to Sarah."

"She won't ever do that. She's prouder than a pea-cock."

"Then it's time she learned a little humility." Day-bright looked ahead and said under his breath, "If we have a real blow, that may teach her a little." His face was stern, and he looked at Josh, a thoughtful light in his eyes. "Nobody feels important when they head into a hurricane. We're all of us mighty small."

"You think it's a *hurricane* up there?" Josh was alarmed. "I've heard they get pretty bad."

The captain repeated, "Nobody feels very big when he's in the midst of a hurricane—not even Dawn Catalina."

5

Hurricane!

I never knew wind could blow this hard!"

The shrill whistling snatched the words from Reb's lips. He knew he had shouted at Dave as loud as he could, but his words sounded feeble and thin.

The two were on deck and had obeyed Daybright's orders to tie themselves down so they wouldn't be washed overboard. Underneath their feet the *Dolphin* plunged up and down in a frightening manner.

Dave looked up to where Captain Daybright was fixed at the wheel, a solitary figure. The others were all below deck.

"I never thought a storm could be this bad," Dave shouted into Reb's ear. "To tell the truth, I'm a little bit scared."

Reb turned his pale blue eyes on his friend. "Ain't nothing wrong with being scared. Right now I don't mind admitting I'm about as scared as a feller can get. Never did like water nohow."

The *Dolphin* bobbed up and down like a wood chip. Overhead the skies were black and ominous. The sea rolled in huge waves. At times the ship would poise on top of a monstrous wave, then would skim down into the trough.

"It's like a blamed rollercoaster!" Reb shouted as they plunged downward. He looked at the wall of water now seemingly as high as the top of the mainmast. "I hope we come out of this!"

Below deck, the Sleepers were clinging to whatever support they could find. In the galley, Jake had tried to fasten everything down, but doors popped open, dishes flew out, and he yelled at Abbey, "Good thing we put that fire out! That's all we need—to have the ship catch on fire."

The *Dolphin* reached the depth of a trough, then rose up at a sharp angle.

Abbey reached over and grabbed Jake's hand. "I'm scared," she cried. Her eyes were large, and her lips trembled. "I think we're all going to die."

Jake held her hand, and they braced their backs against the bulkhead. "We'll be all right. Goél, wherever he is, hasn't forgotten about us," he said. "Don't worry."

Abbey found a faint smile. "Tell me *how* not to worry, and I'll be glad to do it. I've never been in anything like this, Jake."

"Me neither," Jake admitted. He wiped his forehead, and his hand was not steady. "I guess I'll have to admit I'm a little nervous myself."

Josh and Sarah were in the forward compartment with Wash. The three of them had long ago stopped commenting on the storm, but now Josh said, "It's getting worse, I think."

"I don't see how it could get any worse," Wash said. "Those waves are high as a pine tree right now."

"Do you think the ship's going to hold together?" Sarah asked tensely. All wooden ships creaked, but now the *Dolphin* seemed to be nothing but creaks. She looked around, anxious, expecting the water to come in at any moment.

"The captain built it. He said it would stay together," Wash said loyally. "I think it will."

Suddenly Sarah said, "I think I'd better go to Dawn's cabin. She's probably scared to death."

"After what she did to you? Let her be scared," Josh protested.

"No, I'd better go. I know how I'd feel if I were all alone."

Clinging to the bulkhead, Sarah made her way out of the cabin. A sudden shift of the vessel threw her against the wall so that she cried out and fell to the floor. She crawled along the rolling passageway the rest of the way to Dawn's cabin.

She found Dawn lying on her bunk. Faint light streamed in through the porthole, and Sarah asked loudly, "Are you all right, Miss Catalina?"

Dawn Catalina was not all right. She had been in the cabin for several days, speaking to no one. She had taken her meals in silence and refused every offer Sarah had made to patch up the matter.

But this storm was something different! As she turned in the bunk and then sat up, she whispered hoarsely, "What's going to happen?"

Sarah grabbed at the bunk, which was fortunately fastened to both floor and bulkhead. She sat down beside the girl. "We'll be all right."

"I never was in a storm like this before. I—I'm frightened."

"I think we all are," Sarah admitted.

The ship rose and fell again. It seemed to never stop falling, and both girls took deep breaths. Finally the vessel straightened itself, but water suddenly gushed in through the porthole. Sarah looked at it, and fear shot through her. "We'll just have to have faith that we'll be all right," she said as quietly as she could.

"Have faith? Faith in what?"

53

"Why, faith in the ship, faith in Captain Daybright—but mostly faith in Goél. He takes care of his own."

Dawn stared at her blankly and shook her head. "I've heard of Goél. But I've never had faith in anything."

"It might be a good time to begin." Sarah reached out suddenly and seized the girl's hand and held it.

Dawn looked at her in amazement. "Don't you hate me?" she demanded.

"Why, no."

"Well, I . . . I've hated you, and it was all my fault too. I . . . I'm sorry I slapped you."

Sarah smiled and squeezed her hand. "It's all right. We all do things we regret sometimes."

"I do them all the time."

Dawn suddenly began to cry, turning away and putting her face down.

Sarah put her arm around the girl and patted her shoulder. "It's all right. We'll get out of this. Goél knows where we are. Let me tell you about him."

Daybright stared up at the mainmast. The canvas was in ribbons. "We've got to get some kind of sail on her, or we'll founder."

"You mean go up in this kind of weather?" Wash was appalled. The ship was pitching from side to side, and it made his stomach hurt just to think about climbing up the ratlines.

"I'll do it. You hold the wheel."

"No, you'll need help. Dave, come—take the wheel. The captain and I are going to put that sail on the mainmast."

Up the pitching ratlines Wash and Daybright went. They struggled valiantly in the violent gale and finally managed to get enough sail up to catch a wind. When they came down, Dave, at the helm, said, "That's better, Captain," and Daybright knew the rudder had been of no use until the wind in the sail was shoving the ship along.

Daybright stared upward again. It was hard to tell if it was morning or afternoon. The sky was blotted out by a thick cloud cover.

"Do you know where we are, Captain?" Wash asked.

"No. You have to have the sun to know that. Besides, this wind's blown us miles—hundreds of miles, I'd guess—off course." There was a bleak quality in his voice. He had been through difficult times but had never been at the mercy of a storm like this.

All afternoon the *Dolphin* wallowed in the troughs of waves driven by the power of a wind that no man could tame.

"I don't see how we're ever going to find ourselves. If we don't sink, I mean," Josh said.

He looked over at Reb Jackson, who had been seasick for hours. Reb's fighting spirit seemed to be rising again, though. "Never was a horse couldn't be rode," he muttered. He slapped the deck. "We'll ride this one. Don't you worry, Josh."

The *Dolphin* rode out the storm for two more days.

Jake managed to fix enough cold food to make do, for there was no such thing as making a fire. He rattled around in the galley, making sandwiches. He wrapped them in oilcloth and took some to the captain, standing with his feet braced on the deck.

"You have to eat something, Captain! I'll hold her if you want to go below."

Daybright looked at the boy. He was weary to the bone. He had not slept, except in fitful stretches for a few minutes at a time. "No, I'll eat here." He unwrapped a sandwich and bit into it. He found out he was hungry and

55

ate ravenously. When he was through, he said, "That was good, Wash. I'll take the wheel now."

The captain stood by the wheel for hours, it seemed, Wash at his side. Then suddenly Daybright was shouting, "*Look!* Land ahead!"

Wash wiped his eyes free of saltwater and stared into the darkness. "I can't see nothing."

"There! See! Right along the horizon!"

Wash stared hard. "Glory!" he said. "I knew we'd make it."

"We haven't made it yet. Those are rocks, and we're headed right toward them." The captain's voice was tense. "Go tell everybody to put on the warmest clothes they've got and get up on deck. Go by my cabin and bring me some."

"Well, they'll be wet, Captain. Everything's wet."

"That's all right. We can dry out when we hit shore."

Ten minutes later, the Sleepers and Dawn Catalina were on deck. Daybright saw that Dawn's face was as pale as paper. He kept his voice as calm as he could and shouted over the wind. "We're going to hit those rocks." He pointed out over the raging ocean. "No way to dodge them. The ship'll break up, but we'll be all right if we don't lose our heads."

"I can't swim!" Dawn cried. "I'll drown!"

"You stay close to me," he said. "I'll take you in. Can the rest of you swim?"

They could.

"Look around and find something that'll float. The force of the waves will carry you in. Just keep heading for that beach. Hurry now! We're going to hit any minute."

Josh stood beside Sarah. He reached out and took her hand. "Stay with me, Sarah."

She turned a wan smile on him. "It's all right, Josh,"

she said. "We've been through hard times before. Lots of them."

"Sure have. And Goél will help us through this one." He paused, then shouted, "There's the rocks!"

The ship struck with a grinding crash, and the timbers snapped as if they were toothpicks. Everyone was thrown to the deck with the force of the blow.

Daybright yelled, "All right! Over the side. The beach isn't more than forty yards away! Let the waves take you in!" He let go of the wheel and turned, saying, "Come on, Dawn."

"I'm afraid!" she cried. "I always was afraid of water."

Daybright felt sorry for girl. He spoke reassuringly into her ear. "We'll be all right. Just hang onto me." He led her across the deck and saw that the ship was already sinking fast. "Come," he said, "don't fight me. I'll take you ashore."

"Take care of me," she pleaded.

Daybright felt a sudden protective urge come over him. He determined to save this girl if it killed him to do it. "Here we go," he said.

He held her as they jumped off the ship. The water closed over his head, and he hoped she was holding her breath. He came upward with powerful strokes and held her up. He could see her pale face.

"I've got you!" he said. He turned her onto her back, then kicked water until he was moving toward the shore. When his feet touched bottom, he sat her upright. "It's all right now. We're safe."

He helped her to the beach, then said, "Wait here. I'll help the others."

Soon the Sleepers were safely ashore. All gathered in a small group and surveyed the scene. The ship was being torn to pieces by the force of the waves. She was held by the rocks, and the winds seemed to slash at her with mighty fists.

"Well, she was a good ship," Daybright said bleakly as he stared at the vessel he had poured his life into.

"You can build another one, Captain," Wash said, reaching out to take the captain's hand.

Daybright managed a smile. "You're right, Wash. I can always build another one." Then he turned and said, "Come on, folks. We've got to find shelter."

6

"This Here Place Ain't Natural!"

A thin gray light broke over the horizon and cast a feeble gleam on the ocean. The waves were still tossing high, but the fury of the storm had abated.

"Well, I reckon we got thrown up on the shore just like Jonah," Reb said. He tried to smile but shivered, for the night had been cold.

They had all huddled together in their wet clothes, having found no shelter better than a bank that broke the fierce wind.

Daybright stood up and looked out over the sea. "Not much left of the *Dolphin*," he murmured. He saw a few scattered boards and the ribs of the ship, sticking up like a skeleton out of the waves that still pounded her. Turning to the land, the captain stared into the murky light, saying, "I guess we'd better try to find better shelter than this."

"Couldn't we make a fire?" Sarah asked. Her voice shook with the cold, and she hugged herself. "We could dry our clothes out at least."

"I guess we should have brought some supplies, but all I was thinking about was getting us off that ship alive." Daybright looked down at Dawn. "Are you all right, Mistress Catalina?"

"Y-yes," the girl murmured. She hugged herself too, as did the others. "It—it's just cold."

Daybright nodded. "It is for a fact. Let's get off this beach. I hope we find a village or a farm or someplace where there are people."

He was sure that another thought came to several of them at once: *What if there are no people! What if this is a desert island?* No one voiced that thought, however, and they began to trudge through the wet sand.

It was a dismal morning. The wind was still blowing hard, and they had to lean against it to keep from being shoved backward. The sun rose higher, a pale disk visible at last, but there was no sign of any habitation.

"This is about the worst country I've ever seen," Jake muttered. "No sign of anybody living here. Looks like the worst parts of Arizona."

"At least Arizona was warm," Dave argued. "I'd settle for almost anything if I could just get warm."

"Wait a minute! I've got an idea," Wash said. "I can start a fire."

Everyone turned to look at him.

He jammed his hands down in his pants pockets and came out with a small magnifying glass. "If the sun heats up just a little bit, I can get a fire going."

"Everything's wet!" Dave shook his head. "And that sun's not hot enough to make a burning glass any good."

"It'll get hot later," Wash said confidently.

Three hours later the sun was high in the sky, and Wash said, "I'm going to try and make a fire."

Daybright watched him prowl about, breaking off tiny fragments of sticks.

When he saw an old dead tree trunk, a huge one, lying on the ground, Wash said, "That's about the biggest tree I ever saw. It looks like a sequoia. It ought to be dry and rotten down inside."

He broke into the tree trunk and found the inside crumbled to a dry punk. "This is great!" he said. He brought out a handful, brushed away the wet dirt, and made a little mound of the dry material. He gathered his small fragments of sticks close to one side and said, "Now, let's see about this."

He held the glass up to the sun and focused a tiny point of light on the punk. Then he sat down and held his wrist with his left hand so that he could keep it steady. For a time, nothing happened, but then he said, "Look! It's starting to smoke!"

The others crowded around; and sure enough, a tiny spiral of smoke was rising.

"Steady as she goes," Daybright murmured. "I believe you've got something there."

The smoke grew thicker, and suddenly a spark appeared. Carefully Wash blew, and the light grew more prominent. "Come on now, little fire," he breathed, "let's see a little yellow flame there."

As if the fire understood, it suddenly burst into a tiny blaze. A cheer went up, and Wash carefully put the smallest of his sticks over the tiny flame. It caught almost at once. He put the glass down and began adding sticks, very cautiously.

Soon a cheerful fire was going, and the boys were enthusiastically hauling in the driest chunks of wood they could find.

Josh came dragging a huge limb, puffing. "I never saw such a big tree!" he said. "It's enormous." He looked around, and the mist was clearing. "They're all big, though. Look at 'em!"

The Sleepers were not interested in the trees, however, but in getting warm. Most had on at least two sets of clothes, so they arranged branches and dried out one set before the fire. When they were dry, the boys walked off and let the girls change. Then the girls did the same for them.

"Well, it feels better to be dry. Let's go. We'll find somebody. Hope the natives are friendly," Daybright said.

"I just hope they ain't cannibals," Jake muttered.

They continued walking steadily until, perhaps an hour later, Abbey said, "See! See those big bushes. Are those *berries?*"

They ran to where she pointed. Sure enough, bushes higher than their heads were loaded down with berries almost as large as apples.

"Hope they're not poison," Jake said.

"I'll find out." Reb took one of the black berries, bit into it, and chewed for a moment. A grin broke out on his face. "It's too good to be poison," he said. He grabbed another one. "Pitch in. Breakfast is on the table."

The berries were sweet and delicious and, since they all had empty stomachs, brightened their eyes considerably.

"Let's take all these we can with us," Dave said in a practical voice.

They used their extra clothes to make slings and tied them on sticks.

"We look like tramps," Jake said as they started out.

"Are you all right, Miss Catalina?" Daybright asked.

"I'm—yes, I suppose so."

"Your mouth's all smeared with berry juice," he said. He handed her a handkerchief. "Maybe you could wipe it off with this."

Dawn rubbed her lips and stared at the handkerchief. "Thank you," she said, handing it back.

"Better keep it. We may find more berries."

As the group made its way inland, more than anything else Daybright noticed the enormous size of the trees.

"I was in California once," Josh said. "The sequoias were like this, but they were the biggest trees on earth at the time."

Daybright was uneasy. "If this island's deserted," he muttered to Josh, "we'll be in a bad condition."

"Why is that, Captain?"

"Because no ships come this way. I don't know where we are exactly, but it's way off the beaten track. Surely somebody lives here. But not according to the charts."

By midafternoon everyone was very tired. They had seen birds flying high overhead but no sign of animals or people.

Then Reb said, "Come and look at this." He had wandered off to one side, and the others came to where he was pointing down at something.

"What is it?" Abbey whispered.

"It's a footprint—some kind of animal." Reb stared down at it and shook his head. "It sure is a big critter. Look at the size of that thing!"

"That looks like a dog's footprint—but bigger'n any dog I ever saw." Reb put his hands down and spread his fingers out over the track. The print was so big that his hand barely spanned it. He stood up slowly and looked around thoughtfully. "I guess we better be a mite careful from here on. If his feet's that big, I'd hate to think how big his mouth is!"

That thought had occurred to Daybright, and he saw the fear on their faces. "We'd better get on our way," he said quietly.

Reb looked around, back at the footprint, then up at the towering trees. "This here place ain't natural!" he whispered, his voice low and tense.

They made their way into the forest, and the trees covered the sky. It was like walking through a gigantic cathedral. Finally they broke out of the giant forest into a place with smaller trees—not small but seeming so.

"I guess this is the scrub stuff," Dave said, looking about. "I don't know—"

Just then a large animal burst from the trees a hundred yards away.

"Look out!" Daybright yelled. "Take cover!"

"Up this tree!" Josh cried. "All of you!"

Dawn and the Sleepers scurried to the tree, which had limbs growing very close to the ground.

Josh glanced back and saw that Daybright had picked up a club and was waiting. Beyond the captain he saw the animal—a giant dog or wolf—coming at a dead run. He helped Abbey up, then Dawn, saying, "Climb as quick as you can."

Then Josh turned around, picked up a stick, and went to stand beside Daybright.

"Get up that tree, Josh!" the captain ordered.

Josh shook his head stubbornly. "No, I won't do it."

"And we won't either."

They both turned to see Reb, Dave, and Jake armed with heavy sticks.

"All right," Daybright said. "Get close together here. Form a line. Whatever that thing is, he's trouble."

It was a dog, Josh saw, a shaggy creature at least six feet high at the shoulder, rushing at them. The very size of him was awesome.

"Careful now. Maybe we can scare him off."

The dog drew up, baring his fangs and making a rumbling in his throat. He was brownish, short-haired, with huge feet and enormous teeth. But he seemed puzzled by what was in front of him.

"Easy," Daybright said. "I don't think he's seen anything like us before."

The dog hesitated, then leaped forward, jaws open, uttering a roar.

Daybright swung his stick as if he were a baseball player. It whistled through the air and struck the dog on the nose with a satisfying thump. At the same time, Josh's stick struck the animal over the eye, and the other boys fell to clubbing him fiercely, yelling with all their might.

The dog uttered a sharp, piercing yelp and backed up, shaking his head.

"Come on, get him!" Reb yelled.

They charged the beast, and the dog, for all his size, turned tail and ran, uttering shrill yelps.

"We done 'er!" Reb yelled. "By george, by jingo, we showed him who's boss!"

There was much exultation as Daybright and the boys went back to where the three girls were still in the tree.

They climbed down slowly, and Dawn came to stand beside the captain. "That was very brave of you," she said. "He could have killed you."

Daybright flushed but shrugged his shoulders. "I hope he doesn't come back with some bigger friends," he said. "If that's a sample of what's on this island, we're going to have to be more careful."

The wind was still blowing, and before long the skies would be darkening.

"What'll we do, Captain? Camp for the night?" Josh asked, coming up.

"I guess so. You think you can quick make another fire, Wash, while there's still sun?"

"Sure can. I've got the hang of it now." He began at once to scrounge for dry wood with some of the boys helping him.

"Come on, girls, we'll see if we can find some more berries or maybe some nuts. We're going to be mighty hungry," Daybright said.

They searched the woods and did manage to find more berries. They were not as tasty as the first, having a rather bitter tang, but they took all they could carry back to where Wash had gotten a tiny fire started.

Daybright said, "We'd better pull up enough wood to last us through the night. Maybe we can dry out the rest of our clothes—have everything dry by morning."

Everybody was scurrying around, looking for branches to make racks to dry their clothes, when all of a sudden Wash said in alarm, "What's *that?*"

Daybright turned from where he was picking up a chunk of firewood and followed the direction of the boy's gesture. He squinted through the falling darkness and at first could not believe what he was seeing. He blinked, and then Dawn uttered a short cry of fear. He saw that the Sleepers were all staring. He turned his own gaze back and stared with them.

What he saw was what appeared to be a tall shadow moving.

But it's too big to be anything alive, Daybright thought. *It must be a dust cloud.*

But then a final ray of fading sun broke through the clouds, and he saw what he had never dreamed—nor could any of the others.

An enormous man was striding along what seemed to be an invisible road. He was at least two hundred yards away and apparently had not seen them. But even at that distance, Daybright saw it was indeed a living being.

"A—a giant!"

The words escaped Josh's lips. He licked them and said, "Look at him—he must be fifty feet tall."

Sarah gripped Josh's hand. Her voice was thin as she strained to see the disappearing form through the thickening darkness. "Did we dream it?" she said.

"That wasn't a dream—that was a nightmare," Jake whispered. He cleared his throat. "Well, Captain, I guess now we know what the natives are like here."

Daybright nodded slowly. "A land of giants," he said quietly. "We've heard stories from time to time. Sailors would come back and say there was a place like this—but the men were always nearly crazy with fear, so we never believed them."

Dave was looking to where the figure had vanished. "Well, I think you'll have to believe them now, Captain."

7

A Serious Mistake

Daybright decided that they would gamble on keeping the fire going. The night breeze was cold. The after-effects of the hurricane were still whipping in sharp winds.

"The fire's down in a gully," he said. "Nobody can see it—I hope."

They huddled around the blaze. Josh had found a spring of fresh water close by, so they ate all the berries from the first bush and some from the second, and then everyone slaked his thirst.

Then Josh spoke up. "We've seen some strange things in Nuworld: Snakepeople and Gemini Twins—"

"We've even seen a giant," Dave said.

They had indeed met one they called a giant, but he had been no more than eight or nine feet tall.

Dave shook his head. "This is a different kettle of fish altogether."

"At least," Daybright said, trying to put a good face on the thing, "this isn't a deserted island. That would have been the worst of all."

"Why haven't any of the giants from this island ever gone to sea?" Jake wondered. "You say you never heard of any of them?"

Daybright picked up a stick and poked the fire. A log shifted, sending sparks swirling into the darkness that seemed to mingle with the faint stars overhead and then died. The captain shook his head. "No, nothing like this has ever been heard of. Maybe they're not smart enough to build ships—or just don't want to."

"But what about those stories? Did you ever talk to anybody that claimed to have seen them?"

"Just once." Daybright answered Reb's question. "He was old when I met him and was kind of a village joke. He talked about seeing men as tall as trees, but he talked about other wild things too. We all just thought he was crazy."

"I think I'm crazy just looking at one of those creatures," Sarah said, shivering. "They're so huge! Why, if they stepped on one of us, they'd kill us."

"They may be friendly, though," Abbey said quickly. "Just because they're big doesn't mean they're evil."

"That's right," Captain Daybright said, "and at least there's food here. Maybe we could get them to help us build a ship. It'd be easy for them. They could do all the heavy work in no time."

Josh said that somehow he felt a strange dislike for the giants. It was irrational, he knew, and he couldn't explain it. "I don't know. There's something peculiar about all this."

"It ain't natural," Reb agreed. "I think we'd better stay as far away from those giants as we can."

They talked until finally everyone grew sleepy.

"It's a hard situation," Daybright said. "Maybe we can think a little clearer in the morning. Let's all go to sleep now. I guess we'll all have to huddle up together again to stay warm."

He glanced over at Dawn, who had drawn off to one side. He recognized that she felt out of place, a stranger. The Sleepers, of course, were very close, but they didn't deliberately shut her out. *She's probably still ashamed of her behavior*, he thought.

Aloud he said, "Here you go, Mistress Catalina. Plunk down here with the young ladies. You can all stay warm together."

"I guess . . . you can call me 'Dawn.'"

The girl's face was pale. She had not gotten over the shock of the shipwreck and certainly not of seeing the giant. She looked much younger than her eighteen years, he thought as she looked up at him—more like fifteen or sixteen.

As she watched him, he said, "This is harder on you than it is on the rest of us, I'm afraid. Most of us have knocked around a little bit, but you never have, I take it."

"No, I never have." Dawn's voice was small, and she looked out into the darkness as if she were expecting one of the giants to come raging in. "I didn't know it could be like this—to be so afraid."

"We're all afraid at times."

"Not like this." Dawn huddled down, clasping her knees. Her voice was muffled as she said, "I didn't know anybody could be as . . . as afraid as I am now."

Daybright patted her shoulder in friendly fashion. "Things look pretty bleak right now. We're cold and in a strange place with dangers all around. It'll look better in the morning."

Dawn looked up at him, her large green eyes warming. "You always try to say the best things." She sat quietly a moment. "I think about how badly I treated you. I don't see how you can do it."

Sarah had been listening to this. "Come on, Dawn. You can sleep in the middle," she said. "That's what I always wanted to do when I was at a bunking party."

"What's a bunking party?" Dawn asked.

"A sleep-over. It's when a bunch of girls get together and spend the night."

"What did you do?"

"Oh, we drank hot chocolate and watched TV."

"What's hot chocolate—and what's TV?"

"Come on, I'll tell you about it."

71

The girls snuggled together before the fire, and Daybright roamed about, staring into the darkness. Josh and Wash joined him, one on either side.

"What do you think we should do, Captain?" Wash said.

"I don't think we have any choice. We'll have to hope these are friendly folks. We need help getting off this island."

Josh stared into the darkness too. "If they're not friendly," he said, "it's sure going to be one big mess!"

The next morning they ate what was left of the berries and had a conference. All appeared unusually sober, and finally Daybright said, "We're going to have to trust these people. No other choice."

Josh stared at him but said nothing.

They started their journey inland and soon found a wide road, at least forty feet across. It was well worn with wagon tracks and huge footprints.

Sarah came up to walk beside Josh. "You don't think we should make contact with these people, do you, Josh?"

Josh, not wanting to worry her, shrugged. "Oh, it's just a crazy feeling I have. You know how it is. Sometimes feelings are right, sometimes they're wrong."

Sarah was quiet for a while, then said, "If you're right, then we *will* be in trouble. But I suppose there's no help for it."

Thirty minutes later, Captain Daybright called out, "Look! There comes one!"

Josh could not tell if it was the same giant they had seen last night. He was coming from the opposite direction, perhaps on his way home.

"Stand over to one side of the road," Daybright said. "I'd hate for that fellow to step on me."

As the giant came closer, Josh saw he was at least thirty feet tall. He was dressed in some sort of rough, brown clothing and had a thick, rather dull-looking face, a full beard, and dark eyes. He held a staff in his hand and carried a large box by a string.

"We'll have to move to catch his attention. He'd never hear us," Josh said.

When the giant was some distance away, they began waving their arms. His gaze was fixed ahead of him, though. He didn't look down.

Jake quickly picked up a small stone. "Maybe I can get his attention." He flung the stone as the giant approached, and, since Jake was a good shot, it caught the big man on the throat. He slapped at it and muttered something. Then his eye caught the movement of the little people beside the roadway.

The giant stood stock still, staring as if he could not believe his eyes. He actually rubbed his eyes and mumbled something in a rumbling voice.

Josh stopped waving. "Well, he's seen us," he said in a rather fatalistic tone. "I sure hope he likes us."

The giant laid his staff down and knelt before them.

Looking up at him, Josh could not help but feel a start of fear. The giant's huge face loomed over them, and Josh could see the huge, thick hairs of his beard. His eyes were like twin moons, they were so large. His teeth, when he opened his mouth, were discolored, and one had a huge decayed spot on it. He said something again, and his voice came like thunder.

Josh said quickly to the others, "Hold up your hands like this." Then he put his hands out palms upward in the symbol of peace and called out, "We're friends!"

The giant blinked rapidly and looked from one to the other. His mouth dropped open with astonishment. Carefully he put out one finger until it was no more than a foot away from Josh, who was slightly in front.

He advanced it farther, and Josh reached out and tapped it. "Friends!" he yelled. "Friends!"

The giant drew his finger back and sucked on his lower lip. Then he spoke.

When he was through, Josh said, "That's like Middle English—like Chaucer's language. I remember from studying it in school."

"Doesn't sound much like English to me."

"The words are pronounced differently, but I could make out a little of it." He shouted at the giant, using some Middle English words that he remembered.

The big man leaned forward and listened. He nodded vigorously and spoke again.

"It's a lot like Middle English. I liked that when I was in school." Josh shouted back at the giant, who stared at him, then grinned.

"We need help," Josh explained. "Our ship was wrecked." He pointed toward the sea. "We're hungry and tired."

The giant cocked his head to one side. There was a strange light in his eye, but he seemed friendly enough. He pointed down the road and said something.

Even Sarah seemed to understand that he was talking about his house. She said, "He wants us to go home with him, doesn't he?"

"I think so." Josh cupped his hands and shouted, "Take us with you, please."

The giant nodded. Then he said in his big voice, "Too far away. I will carry you." He opened the box that he had been toting by a string. Carefully he reached down and picked up Josh.

As the huge fingers closed around him, the boy nearly panicked. It was a terrifying feeling.

74

The giant held him even with his eyes, stared at him, then nodded again. "Home!" he said, then lowered him into the box. One by one the giant picked up the Sleepers. Last, he picked up Daybright and Dawn and deposited them in the box. Then he fastened the top on.

Inside the box it was foul smelling and dirty.

Daybright was holding Dawn's hand. "We're all right," he kept saying. "He's friendly. There's no other way to get us where we're going, although this is pretty foul."

"What was in this box?" she asked. "It smells terrible."

"I think it's tobacco," Josh said. He felt around, touched something, pulled off some of it, smelled it. "That's what it is—some kind of tobacco."

"Well, we're on our way," Reb said cheerfully. "We're not going to starve to death, and if any of us want to take up smoking, there's enough tobacco here to do the job."

It was dark inside the box. It also swung about in an alarming manner as the giant walked.

Finally Reb cried out, "This is worse than being on a ship!"

Daybright agreed, and Dawn clung to him pitifully. "It'll be all right," he called out to everyone. "We'll be out of this soon. You'll see."

It was hard to judge the time, but finally they heard the giant speak to someone, and a voice answered. They heard the sound of his footsteps on what seemed to be steps. Then the box was slammed down, throwing them all to their knees.

"I guess we're here," Daybright said and looked up as the top of the box disappeared.

The light came flooding in, blinding Josh for a moment. Then he saw a woman's huge face peering over the side.

The woman screamed slightly. "What are they, Gant?"

Josh understood this sentence and got to his feet. He waved at the woman. "That must be his wife," he said, "and his name must be Gant. Hello, Mrs. Gant," he called out.

When the woman heard her name in Josh's tiny voice, she clamped a hand over her mouth and stepped back.

At once another face appeared. This time it was the face of a girl—a giant girl. She stared at them.

No more than ten or twelve, Josh thought.

"Hello," Daybright called, waving. "How are you, little girl?"

The girl giggled and poked her finger down toward him.

Daybright reached out and touched the finger but could not get his hand around the end of it. He pulled off his cap and bowed gracefully, saying, "My name is Daybright. What's yours?"

She did not appear to understand him, but her father did. "Tell the Little People your name."

The girl stared back, then smiled. She had bright teeth that looked very large. "Olina," she said.

Suddenly the girl reached into the box and snatched up Sarah.

Sarah gave a cry of alarm. She kicked and gave a little scream, which seemed to delight the girl.

Olina said, "Nama?"

"She wants to know your name," Josh yelled. "Tell her."

"My name is Sarah!" Sarah shouted.

The girl squealed. "Sarah!" she said. With her free hand she touched Sarah's clothes in wonder. "Sarah!" she repeated.

"Put her down," Gant said. "You might hurt her."

Gant reached into the box, carefully lifting out the

76

rest of the party one by one. Soon all were standing on a tabletop, and Josh had a chance to look around.

It was a typical farmhouse scene. In a huge fireplace at one end was a black pot containing some kind of bubbling stew. There was rough wooden furniture, all handmade. There was only one window to let in light.

Gant spoke rapidly to his wife, telling her how he had found the "Little People."

Josh discovered he was quickly remembering his Middle English. When Gant turned back, he motioned until the giant leaned toward him. "Could we have something to eat?" he shouted. "We're hungry."

Gant turned to his wife and said, "Feed them."

She looked at them and asked, "In what?"

It was a problem, but they managed to find what was presumably the smallest vessels they had.

Josh and Sarah moved to one side of a bowl of stew, while Dave and Jake got on the other side. "Well, we don't have any spoons," Josh said, "so I guess we'll do the best we can."

The stew contained some sort of meat and vegetables and was actually very good.

Dawn, eating at another bowl beside Daybright, suddenly looked down at her hands and laughed. "I never ate like this before," she marveled, "but it's so good."

"It is a little messy—" Daybright grinned "—but we'll make the best of it. And it *is* good stew."

After they had eaten, the giant and his family pulled up chairs, and for a long time, with much shouting, Josh tried to explain where they had come from. But he turned finally and shrugged his shoulders. "It's no use. They think this island is the whole world. They can't imagine there being another place—especially with strange little people in it like us."

"Ask him if he'll help us get away. We'll need a ship," Daybright asked.

When Josh asked the question, Gant cricked his head to one side. "A ship? What is a ship?"

"This is going to be harder than I thought," Daybright muttered. "Tell him it's something you get into and go on the water."

Josh did his best to explain, and Gant seemed to understand a little better. After the giant spoke for quite a while, Josh said, "I think they have little boats here, maybe for their rivers. Of course, they'd be big to us. I don't think they have any ocean-going vessels, though."

"That's bad news. Ask him if he can help us build one."

This was a difficult concept to get across, but at last Gant said that he would help. At least that's what Josh thought he said.

It was getting late, and they were very tired.

Gant said, "We will fix you a place to stay."

The "place" turned out to be a cage. It was clean though, and Olina seemed to take great pleasure in making them beds out of rags.

When Josh protested that they didn't want to sleep in a cage, Gant pointed over to a corner where an enormous cat was watching with slitted green eyes.

"Cat would think you were a mouse—eat you." The giant laughed heartily, and the force of his laughter nearly knocked Josh off the table.

"Well, then, I guess it's all right."

"But, please," Sarah asked, "could you put up a piece of something so that the girls could have one part of the cage, Olina?"

Olina understood finally what she was asking, and she got her father to put a piece of thin board most of the way across the middle of the cage. Then the giant girl pointed at the extra clothes that the Sleepers had brought with them. She said, "I will wash clothes."

"Well, that's nice of her," Abbey said. She gave her extra dress to the girl, and the others handed over their bundles of clothing.

Olina beamed. "I will wash very nice," she said.

Finally the giants went to bed, and the Sleepers were left alone.

The partition was in place, but the young men were very much aware of the girls around the corner.

"Don't worry," Daybright called. "We'll get out of this all right."

Josh was sitting with his back against the board. He knocked on it. "Sarah? You there?"

Sarah, on the other side, tapped and said, "Yes."

Josh said, "Well, here we go again. We've been in lots of jails, but these jailers are a little bit different."

The two talked quietly, but, since everyone could hear them, they had little personal to say.

Finally Dawn said, "They're so *big*. I'm afraid of them."

"It's all relative," Jake said airily. "Don't you worry, Miss Dawn. They're nice folks. You see how the girl's washing our clothes for us."

Something seemed to be bothering Abbey, though. "Yes," she said, "but she thinks we're like dolls. I don't think they're able to think of us as people at all. There's too much difference."

Wash thought for a while and said, "Well, that does make a problem. When people are different, they have a hard time understanding each other."

But finally all settled down to sleep, and the last thing Josh remembered was being held high in the air, looking into the eyes of a giant.

79

8
The Little People

Well, we're not going to starve to death, that's for sure."

The Sleepers and the captain, with Dawn at his side, sat at the makeshift table that Olina had made for their use. It was a board placed on two blocks, and it was set on the large table that served the family. The seats were bits of wood.

"At least," Josh said, "we don't have to eat out of the same bowl."

Olina was bringing their food. She glowed as she bent over with a huge bowl of scrambled eggs. After putting it down, she took the bits of wood that Reb had carved into round shapes and carefully put a spoonful of eggs on each.

Reb picked up his spoon and waved it. "Why, shoot! This ain't half bad," he said. "Always did like scrambled eggs."

Olina smiled at the boy. She leaned over so close that her face looked enormous. Then she hovered nearby, watching.

The group ate, breaking off chunks of the piece of bread that Olina had put before them.

When they had finished, Sarah stood up and smiled, waving her hand at the giant child. "Olina! We're so dirty. Could you possibly fix us something to take a bath in?"

"Bath?" The girl thought hard, then nodded. "Yes. I will fix it."

"Well, this is liable to be embarrassing." Sarah laughed

shortly. "She may want to plunk us all down in one big bowl and wash us as she would a doll."

It proved not to be that difficult, however. Olina obviously had learned that Little People girls needed their privacy from Little People boys. She came back with two long, deep cooking pans. Quickly she piled boxes between the two pans, forming a sort of curtain. Then she brought a kettle of water and filled each pan to the top.

"Hot!" she warned.

"Do you have any soap—and maybe something to dry off on?" Abbey shouted.

Olina smiled. She came back with a large chunk of strong-smelling white soap and broke it in two, putting half beside each pan. One more trip served to bring some cloths that would do as towels and washcloths.

Placing the three girls on their side, she nodded. "I wash your other clothes." She took the clothes and disappeared.

"Well, this is about as much privacy as we are going to get," Abbey said. "I feel so dirty. That water looks good to me." She reached over the lip of the huge pan to check the temperature. "Just right." She grinned. "Last one in's a rotten egg."

It was a strange time for Dawn Catalina. She was far more accustomed to having her bath drawn by servants and then her back being scrubbed by maids. Afterward, she would step out onto a soft rug and be dried with fluffy towels.

Not so this time! She was dirty and gritty, including her hair, which was stiff with saltwater. But soon she was in the pan, which was as large as some swimming pools, and the three girls were laughing and splashing water on each other. The soap was strong and far too large, but they managed to break off enough to work up a nice lather. Then they helped each other wash their hair.

Sarah noticed that Dawn had relaxed a great deal in their company, and she thought, *I think this experience might be good for her—if we get out of it. Make her a little bit more democratic.*

Across the barricade, the boys splashed and sputtered and washed and had just pulled on their clothes when Olina's huge moonlike face appeared.

"She don't give a guy much privacy," Jake muttered.

But she had a set of their clothes washed and dried.

"You girls all right?" Jake yelled.

Sarah's voice came back. "Yes. How about you?"

"Cleaner'n a whistle."

"Well, what do we do with ourselves now? We've eaten and had our baths." Josh walked to the edge of the barricade and met Sarah, who was trying to comb out her hair with her fingers. "You're going to have a tangled mess," he said. "You need a brush."

"I know it," Sarah said. "We all do. Do you think Reb might whittle us a comb of some kind out of some wood? Anything would do."

Reb was prevailed upon, and he did manage to make a comb of sorts. It was thick and awkward, but the three girls shared it and soon were looking fairly presentable.

Then Olina appeared suddenly again with a huge box in her hands. Without asking permission, she reached down and scooped up Jake.

"Hey! Put me down!"

Olina did put him down—inside the box. The others were immediately placed in the box as well, and Olina said, "We go play now."

"I guess we don't have any choice," Dave said, holding onto the side of the carton.

Olina held the box before her and went outside, where the sun was shining and the clouds were white against the blue sky. She set down the box underneath a towering tree; then one by one she picked up the Little People and set them on the ground.

"This grass is high," Dave complained.

The grass was nearly up to their chests. It was worn flat around the giants' cabin, however, and for a time they explored.

"Hey! Look at this," Reb called.

Everyone came running and saw that he had found a huge beetle creeping along. It was higher than his head and at least six or eight feet across.

"Oh, it looks awful," Abbey said.

"Naw, it looks like fun." Reb grinned. He leaped on the beetle's back and began kicking the hard armored side with his heel. "Get up! Let's go! Have a little speed here!"

The others laughed, and Josh shook his head. "Reb, I believe you'd try to ride anything."

The young Southerner grinned. "Well, this thing's got two more feet than most hosses—but anything for a ride."

They watched for a while, then all took turns riding the beetle. It seemed placid enough and lumbered along safely.

Olina hovered over them, shutting out the sun sometimes with her shadow. Her laughter sounded like thunder.

After a while she took them down to a creek and set them down.

"This thing's wider than the Mississippi River—to us anyway," Dave marveled.

It was a beautiful stream, though—clear water ran over rounded rocks—and Wash said, "Let's go fishing."

The idea caught fire at once, and they spent a considerable amount of time obtaining the proper gear. Olina, at their request, found thread, which furnished the line. Her mother had some sharp pins, which, by great effort, Reb bent into hooks.

When they had cut the smallest saplings they could find, Reb said, "But what'll we use for bait?"

Wash looked about. "I don't know . . . the worms here'd be big enough to eat us, almost. Let's just ask Olina for some of that stew meat that we had yesterday."

The girls didn't want to fish, but the boys all clamored to go. Finally out on a grassy bank, they baited their hooks and threw them in.

The current carried the lines downstream, and almost at once Wash's cork, which was nothing but a piece of wood, disappeared with a *plop*.

"I got one!" he yelled. "I got one!" The line zipped through the water, and his pole bent double. "It must be a whale!" he said excitedly. He struggled with the fish, and everyone gathered around, calling encouragement.

Finally Wash backed up and, with a mighty heave, dragged the fish up on the shore.

"That thing must weigh twenty pounds!" he cried. "Look at it!"

"Some kind of a perch, I guess. One of the little ones," Reb said. He picked up a stick and knocked the fish on the head so that it would stop flopping. "That's enough to feed all of us." he said.

They fished all afternoon, spread up and down the bank. Sometimes fish that were simply too big and powerful grabbed line and pole and dragged them off.

Josh jerked up his head when he heard a wild scream from one of the girls.

Throwing his pole down, he ran full speed, joined by the other boys. When he passed over a small knob of earth, he saw that Dawn was faced by a frighteningly large snake that was coiled and had its beady eyes fixed on her.

Josh hesitated. If there was anything he didn't like and was afraid of, it was snakes! He knew the others were awed by the size of the reptile too. It must have been at least thirty feet long and had a wicked look about it.

Then Captain Daybright suddenly appeared and, without breaking stride, got between the girl and the hissing serpent. It made a picture that Josh would ever forget—the huge, green snake with beady eyes and fangs exposed and Daybright standing there, his blue eyes flashing. He had a staff in his hand, his only weapon.

"Get away from here, Dawn," he said under his breath.

Breathing hard, she began to back off.

The serpent, sensing its prey leaving, drew back its neck in a striking coil.

Daybright was holding the staff by one end. He held the other out toward the snake—a pitiful weapon but all that he had.

"He's gonna strike! Watch out, Captain!" Wash yelled.

The snake's strike came like a flash. The head flew forward, fangs out, ready to impale the stalwart sailor.

The snake had timed its strike perfectly; but instead of the fangs burying themselves in flesh, the staff caught the reptile directly on the nose and broke its strike. At once Daybright swung the staff in a mighty sweep. It came smashing down on one of the snake's eyes, which dulled immediately. With a hiss the serpent coiled backward, writhing.

At the same moment, a huge stick came down from above and crashed onto the snake.

Josh looked up to see the girl Olina, her eyes flashing as she wielded her club again and again. "Bad snake!" she said.

"Look out! She's fainting!" Sarah called.

Captain Daybright turned to see Dawn Catalina slowly

86

collapsing. Dropping the staff, he scooped her up and carried her quickly away from the dying snake.

Lowering her to the grass, he said, "Dawn, are you all right?" He pushed her hair back, an anxious look on his face.

Her face was pale. She lay in his arms for a moment as the others gathered around.

"Is she all right?" Josh asked.

"I think so—just fainted," Daybright answered.

Dawn came to herself after a few moments. She seemed confused. But the first face she saw was that of Daybright, looking down at her anxiously, and for the first time she called his name. "Daybright," she said, and then she started, as though memory of the snake had come back.

"It's all right. It's dead. How do you feel?"

Dawn's cheeks flushed as she found herself being held in Daybright's strong arms. "I'm . . . I'm all right." She looked up at him and whispered, "You saved my life."

Daybright flushed as well. "I guess Olina saved both our lives." He waved an arm at the giant girl. "Thanks!" he shouted.

Olina bent over. "You all right, Little Woman?"

"Yes." Dawn smiled and got to her feet rather shakily. "I'm all right. Thank you, Olina."

"We'd better go play somewhere else," she announced solemnly. "Snakes are bad."

Olina led her little troop away to a pond, where she found a flat board. It made a nice boat for two. Wash rigged up a mast and sail, and they spent the rest of the afternoon going around the smooth pond.

They saw no more snakes, and Dawn stayed very close to Daybright's side.

"Look at the size of those ducks," she said. "They're huge."

"Not in this world," Daybright said. "They *would* be in our world." He admired the white feathers of the ducks, and when the birds flew off, he said, "We could almost ride on those."

Dawn laughed shortly. "No, thanks. I've had enough adventures for a while."

"This has been hard on you, Dawn. I know you're not used to such things."

She shook her head. "It's been hard on all of us," she said simply. Then her face darkened. "I'll never forget that snake. It would have killed me sure, if you hadn't come. How could you ever face it?"

"It was no more dangerous than a storm at sea." Daybright put the matter aside and looked at her, laughing and changing the subject. "I'll bet you've never gone so long without a new dress in all your life, have you?"

Dawn looked down at her dress, which was wrinkled and torn in several places. "You know," she said thoughtfully, "it doesn't seem to matter as much anymore. I guess everything is seen in comparison with something else. Back home I had so many new things I didn't appreciate any of them. That's how life is. When you have so much, you just don't appreciate it."

"Hunger makes a good appetite," the captain said. "When you're full, nothing tastes really good; but when you're hungry, one egg is the best thing in all the world."

They sat talking for a long time until finally Olina called, "Time to go home!" As the giant girl wrapped her chubby hands around them and lifted them up, Daybright grinned and winked at Dawn. "I guess you can get used to anything—even being picked up by a child in one hand."

For the rest of that week, Olina made clothes for all her guests. They were made of the finest cloth she could find, but when Dawn put hers on, she laughed outright.

"It's like dressing in a blanket," she exclaimed. But she thanked Olina for it, curtsying, and the girl's face beamed.

They couldn't really wear the clothes, and Abbey said, "She's just playing dolls with us like I did with my dolls at home, dressing them. I haven't thought of my Barbie dolls in a long time. I must have had twenty of them."

"I did too," Sarah confessed, "and all other kinds of dolls as well."

They had grown fond of Olina. Her mother was there from time to time, watching curiously, but it was the young girl who cared for them, saw that they were fed and safe from the cat. She put them in the cage each night, for the cat did roam loose.

They all received a shock one night when Wash looked down and saw in the moonlight something that startled him. "Look at that!" he said.

Reb had been sleeping beside him. He crawled up and looked through the slats of the cage. What he saw was a huge brown rat. "That thing's bigger'n any dog I ever saw," Reb breathed. "Look at those teeth!" It was an evil-looking creature, and Reb shivered. "I'd just as soon be in this cage as out there with him."

"Where'd he come from?"

"Well, this house ain't too well built. He could've come in anywhere." When Reb later spotted a hole near the floor, he said, "I reckon the rat came from there. I wish they'd set a rattrap. I don't fancy having that scoundrel around. Never could stand rats!"

Breakfast was interrupted one morning as Gant came to watch Olina feed her charges. He observed closely as they ate, and then he turned about and began to speak.

"These Little People," Gant said in a voice of thunder, "are going to make us rich."

"What do you mean, Papa?" Olina asked. She looked fondly at the Little People. "What are you going to do?"

"I'm going to sell them to rich people."

A chill went down Daybright's spine. He knew that most of the Sleepers, except for Josh, could understand little of the giants' language, but everybody appeared to understand that. Daybright and Dawn stared at each other in shock.

"They're worth lots of money." A crafty look came to Gant's thick face. "I'm going to take two of them." He leaned over the table, and his eyes went from one to another. Finally he said, "I'll take these two." His huge hands reached down, and he plucked up Dawn and the captain.

His hands had a greasy feel and smelled terrible. Dawn began to cry, and Daybright struggled, but of course it was useless.

Holding them high, Gant stared at the two. "I'll take these. You teach the rest to sing and dance."

"Don't take them, Papa. They'll be lonesome by themselves away from their friends."

"They're not people," Gant said in surprise. "They're pets. You always cry over pets. When we ate your pet chicken, you cried for a week. No, I've got to have money."

Ignoring the pleas of his daughter, he put Daybright and Dawn in a carrying box. It was padded and had air holes punched in it, large enough to admit light. Still, when the top closed down, Dawn grabbed for Daybright and held onto him.

"What's going to happen to us?" she whispered.

Daybright did not answer. He had been in storms at sea and had faced many other dangers, but nothing in his experience was like this. He tried to think of a way to escape, but as the box swayed back and forth and he heard the giant saying good-bye to his family, he felt they had seen the last of the Sleepers.

He sat down beside Dawn, and she fell against him. He held her, comforting her as he would a child. She was weeping, and he thought, *Sometimes I wish a man could cry. It's about all I know to do in a fix like this.*

9

Sold to the Highest Bidder

For Dawn Catalina the journey from Gant's cottage to the city must have been one of the most terrifying events she'd ever known. Their prison admitted light through the holes, and Daybright was grateful for that. Total darkness would have been far too frightening for her. She clung to him, holding his big hand with both of hers as if she were a frightened child.

The box rose up and down regularly as their giant captor swung along the road. After a time Daybright heard his big voice rumbling, and then they were jolted rudely as he shifted the box.

By peering out one of the airholes, Daybright could see that apparently Gant had climbed onto a wagon. "I can see horses," he reported, sitting back down. "Monsters they are, like everything else in this blasted place!"

Instantly he regretted speaking harshly. *The girl's frightened enough,* he thought. Aloud he said cheerfully, "Well, look at it this way, Dawn. I thought we'd never get out of the *Dolphin* alive when that storm hit—but we did. Then, we had snake problems, and we got out of that. We've just got to have faith that we'll make it."

Dawn looked up at him quickly. "Sarah talks about faith—faith in Goél—but I don't have any. I've never had to."

"I guess wealthy folks don't need it—or don't think they do."

"They do, though. They're just like everybody else."

Daybright laughed suddenly. "I'll bet you never said *that* before." He looked at her, grinning. "When's the last time you said, 'Those poor peasants out there are just like me'?"

Dawn seemed to catch the humor of his remark. "I guess I never did," she said.

Suddenly the box gave a violent jolt as the wagon evidently hit a pothole, jarring Daybright so that his teeth ground together.

"Oh!" Dawn moaned. "This is terrible. But you are right," she continued. "I guess I do see things differently since being in this place. I'm really not very important after all."

"Because you're small?"

"Why, yes."

Daybright thought for a moment, then he said, "Size doesn't mean anything. I knew a fellow once who was almost seven feet tall, a giant of a fellow. A giant in our world, that is. He was a good friend of mine, good at games, a hard worker. Not very much upstairs, but a nice fellow.

"I had another friend who was tiny, not over five two or three, smart as a whip, always willing to help. Would you say he was worth less than the big man?"

"Why, no, of course not."

"So being an important person is not a matter of inches. It's a matter of what's on the inside, and you've got more on the inside than that hulk of a Gant who's hauling us around. So that makes you important."

Dawn managed a smile. "It sounds nice when you say that, Daybright."

"Why don't you call me Ryland?" he said suddenly. "I feel like a servant or something when you call me by my last name."

"All right—Ryland. That's a nice name." Dawn smiled. "I like it."

"It was my father's name. It'll be my son's too."

"Oh!" Dawn said. "You're married then?"

"No, I'm not married."

"But—about a son?"

"Oh, well, I'll have one someday—and daughters too. And you know what?"

"What?"

"I hope they have red hair like yours. I always liked red hair—hated mine."

"Your hair's very nice," Dawn said quickly.

Daybright kept the conversation going, mostly to keep up Dawn's spirits, and then finally he felt the wagon draw to a stop. "I guess we're here," he said. "This is going to be hard."

"They won't separate us, will they?"

"I hope not." In his heart he was not at all sure. He knew that Gant would take the best offer made for them, and the thought of being cut off from his own kind forever brought a wrench. He knew that Dawn was thinking the same thing. "We'll be all right. Remember Goél. He knows how to help people in trouble. Trust him."

"All right, Ryland," she said, "I'll try."

The box was yanked up, and the giant's voice boomed. They began moving again. Daybright heard Gant's heavy footsteps as he went up stairs and down long corridors. Then their prison was set down with a shock that drove both Daybright and Dawn to their knees.

"This is it," Daybright said. "Remember, don't let them see you show fear."

"All right, Ryland, I'll try," she said again.

There was considerable talking, and by looking through one of the air holes, Daybright could see what was going on. "It looks like he's gathered a group of prospective buyers."

"I've heard of slave markets, but I never thought I'd be involved in one," Dawn whispered.

At that moment, the box lid was lifted, and Gant called out loudly, "Look! Here they are—the miracle I told you about. See them!" Reaching down, he seized Daybright and Dawn and lifted them high.

Accustomed as Daybright was to climbing tall masts that moved erratically in the winds, the sudden sweep upward caused him a moment's dizziness. He was held from the waist down in the grip of the giant's huge hand, and as he looked around he saw a room filled with other giants wearing expensive-looking robes and jewelry that glittered. He observed quickly that in the ring on one of Gant's fingers was a diamond at least four inches across. *That'd bring a king's ransom back in my country,* he thought grimly and then forced himself to be still.

Holding the captives high, Gant began his spiel. His sales pitch was that you can buy very few things that are rare. These Little People were the only ones of their kind.

Dawn, held in the giant's other fist, glanced over at Daybright. "He's lying," she said. "Why?"

"To get more for us," he said. "But don't try to interrupt him."

This would have been impossible, for at once an auction began. Daybright was familiar with village streets where vendors sold their wares, calling out their prices and arguing loudly with those who passed by—prospective buyers. Apparently these giants were used to such haggling over price. The sound of their voices was like thunder, and after a time Dawn put her hands over her ears.

From time to time, one of the prospective buyers was allowed to hold them. One, an elderly giant with long skinny fingers, picked Dawn up and held her close to his nearsighted eyes. His beard was like pack ropes, and he had large eruptions on his face that made him repulsive. He prodded her with his forefinger and grunted. "Twenty-two gold pieces. My highest offer."

Gant snatched Dawn back and laughed loudly. "You're always searching for a bargain, sir, but that's not enough."

How long the bargaining went on, Daybright was not quite sure. But then a sudden silence came over the room. Gant placed his captives down on a table and tapped them with his finger to make them move about.

Daybright looked up to see the crowd parting to make an aisle. Down the aisle strolled a man dressed in a blue robe with a massive gold chain around his neck and a crown on his thick white hair. He had a proud, lean face, and his voice broke over the room. "I have come to see your wares, Gant. I hear you have something unusual."

"Indeed, Sire. Look!"

Gant pointed at his captives. "Have you ever seen anything like this, My King?"

The king's sharp black eyes fixed on Daybright and Dawn. He advanced and stood over them. His lips drew into a tight line as he studied the pair. "Where did you find them?" he asked.

"Close to the ocean. I think the sea washed them in."

"There must be others," the king said.

The giant shrugged his mountainous shoulders. "Perhaps, but they would be far away in another land."

The king hesitated only for a moment. "I will take them."

"But—but the price, My King . . ."

The king shrugged. "You will have thirty pieces of gold. I'll take them with me now."

"But—but they're worth more, Your Majesty!"

The king put his piercing eyes on Gant, who seemed to shrivel up.

Gant cried, "No . . . I mean . . . thank you, Your Majesty, for your kindness."

"See that you keep a civil tongue in your head." The king picked up Daybright and Dawn, one in each hand. His fingers squeezed so hard that both of them gasped. "You'll be a nice addition to my little museum," he said.

Daybright shouted, "Your Majesty, you must listen to me."

The king's eyes opened in surprise. "They talk! Well, it's to be expected. Do you sing?"

"No, I don't sing."

"Do *you* sing?" The king lifted Dawn higher.

"Y-yes, yes," she stammered. "I sing a little."

"Good. I will have my dancing master teach you to dance. Then you can perform for me and my guests." Without another word he put them down into the box and closed the lid.

The darkness closed in again, and Daybright felt the box sway upward as they began the journey to the palace.

After the king left, Gant took his payment from the king's steward. He gloated over the gold, feeling the smooth surface of the coins, then slipped it all into a leather bag.

"Not enough, though!" A crafty look touched his eyes, and he thought, *I'll make more from the rest of them. There be some that be as rich as the king. I'll sell them off one at a time. They'll fetch more that way.*

He left the village and started down the road. "This is the last time I'll go afoot," he said. "I'll buy me horses and a carriage and go like the gentry do!"

10

"We're Not Animals!"

Sarah awoke just before dawn to find the other Sleepers awake too. They had gone to bed early, had slept well, and now that early morning light was coming through the window, they were restless.

"We'd better have a talk before Olina gets here," Josh said. He stretched and stood to his feet, holding onto the slats of their cage. Even as he did he exclaimed, "There's one of those rats again. I can't stand those things!"

"I expect most houses in this place have rats," Jake said. "They're what brought the Black Plague on, you know. Killed about one-fourth of Europe."

"Jake, you say the awfulest things!" Sarah snapped. "Can't you think of anything pleasant to talk about?"

"I don't know anything pleasant about rats, do you?" Jake growled angrily. He was irritable—as were the rest of them, Sarah noted—and now cast a discontented look at Josh. "We've got to do something! Sooner or later we've got to break out of this place."

"That's fine with me," Josh said angrily. "What's your master plan for getting us out of here?"

"I'm not the leader. You are."

"Please don't quarrel," Abbey said. "I know it's hard, and we're all worried—but there's no sense fighting one another."

Sarah turned to look at Abbey, a smile on her face. She thought how the girl had changed since the Sleepers' last dangerous encounter where she had offered to give up her beauty for the sake of the others.

"Abbey's right," she said. "We can't quarrel among ourselves."

Jake ducked his head and muttered, "I'm sorry. I guess my nerves are a little bit stretched."

"Well, mine are too," Reb said. "I feel like the time I was in the pokey for stealing hogs with my Uncle Seedy."

"You stole hogs?" Dave exclaimed.

"Well, no, I didn't. My uncle did. I was just along to help him load them."

"Well, that makes you as guilty as he was, doesn't it?" Wash said.

"What are you talking about? He stole 'em, I loaded 'em." Reb's voice contained hurt innocence. "It's not against the law to load a hog—only if you steal him."

"I guess we'd better not get into the ethics of hog stealing right now," Josh said. He turned and stared at the rat, which was disappearing into its hole. Then he turned back to face his friends. "We've got to escape all right— get away from this place."

"And what would we do then?" Dave asked. He had a practical streak in him. "We'd probably get eaten by a snake or a wolf or something. Going out there is like going into a zoo with the animals all loose."

"It would be better than staying here," Reb insisted. "At least we'd have a chance. And I'm getting tired of being treated like a doll."

"Olina's a sweet girl," Abbey spoke up at once. "She just doesn't understand that we are people and not toys."

"That's right." Sarah nodded. "I think she's our only hope. We've got to try to persuade her to let us go."

"She'd never do that," Reb said. "We're just like her toys. Besides, she'd be afraid of her father."

Finally Olina and her mother got up, and soon the Sleepers were eating breakfast—oatmeal and chunks of bread smeared with butter. Reb had whittled not only eating utensils for all of them but also trenchers to hold their food.

Olina was delighted as always to see her Little People. She had learned all of their names, and they had become accustomed to her speech.

In the middle of the morning she took them outside. She was very careful where she let them play, for she had learned there were many enemies that could destroy her pets.

As the Sleepers strolled around in the chest-high grass, Jake pointed out an anthill. The ants were huge, almost a foot long, and Reb cautioned him, "Don't get those things stirred up, Jake. I bet they could bite pretty hard. Little old fire ant back in the old days could hurt like blazes. I'd hate to think what one of these could do."

They were interested in watching the ants, however, giving Sarah a chance to talk to Olina. She had grown fond of the giant girl, and Olina had made a special pet of her.

"Olina, I've got to talk to you!" she shouted.

"All right." Olina lay full length on the grass and turned her face upward.

Her skin, smooth as it was, looked rough when viewed through Sarah's eyes. Sarah thought suddenly, *If you enlarge anything, it looks worse.* She remembered seeing a piece of fine silk through a microscope. It had looked like a tattered, rough, ugly blanket. So it was with the features of all the giants.

"Olina, I want to talk to you about us."

Olina nodded. "I like you," she said. "I'm so glad you came."

"I'm glad that you like us, but there's something you've got to understand."

"What's that, Sarah?"

101

"Well, because we're small compared to you, you think of us as dolls or perhaps as one of your pets."

Olina loved pets. She had several birds in cages, and a puppy, and kittens in the barn that she was not allowed to bring into the house.

"Yes, but you're my favorites of all," she said.

"But Olina," Sarah said desperately, looking very serious. "Can't you see that I'm different from your puppy or from one of your birds?"

"Oh, yes, I see that." Olina smiled, nodding. She reached her finger out and carefully stroked Sarah's hair. "You're a lot smarter than them. They can't talk like you can."

Sarah felt a moment's helplessness wash over her. How was she to get the concept of her humanity into the head of this young girl who had never seen anything like the Sleepers?

Taking a deep breath, she said, "Olina, suppose someone took you to town and you were sold and the people made a pet out of you. What would you think?"

"I wouldn't like it. That would be awful."

"It *is* awful. That's what I'm trying to tell you."

Olina's brow wrinkled. She rolled over on her side and supported her head with her hand, keeping her blue eyes fixed on Sarah. Some thought seemed to trouble her. "You don't like me?"

"Oh, yes, I do like you, Olina. We all do. You take care of us so well. But you take care of your puppy and your kittens out in the barn the same way. And we're not like them."

"What do you mean, Sarah?"

"I mean, we're not animals—we're people, just like you are."

"Oh, we're a *lot* different."

"No, you aren't—except in size. When you hurt your thumb yesterday, it hurt." She held up her own thumb and said, "When I hurt mine, it hurts too. Sometimes you get lonesome; so do I. You have good friends, and so do I. I'm just smaller than you are."

That seemed to be a new thought to the giant child. She pursed her lips and frowned slightly. "But you're not like us."

For the next twenty minutes Sarah did her best to get through to the girl, but it seemed to be a hopeless matter.

Finally Olina went as far as she knew how. "You're my friend, Sarah," she said. "I love you."

There was such charm in the young giantess, though she was huge and sometimes clumsy, that Sarah could not help but smile. "I love you too, Olina. I'd do anything for you. So we're friends."

Later on that evening, Sarah and Josh were watching while Olina and her mother cooked supper. "I tried to talk to Olina today about how we're people, just like she is."

"I don't think you'll ever get her to understand that."

"I suppose not. She's sweet, but as far as she's concerned we're just toys or pets, little dolls for her to play with."

"Well, she's never seen anything like us. I don't know what I would have thought if a person six inches high would have popped up on my doorstep." He nudged Sarah. "Maybe I would have sold him at the county fair."

"No, you wouldn't. You're not like that, Josh."

The two of them sat there quietly. They had been friends a long time and had learned that friends didn't have to talk all the time. Once Josh had said, "Sarah, it's nice to be around you. You don't talk all the time like other girls."

Sarah had been angry until she realized that he was paying her a compliment.

"What do you suppose is happening to the captain and Dawn?" Josh asked.

"I'm worried about them. What if they separated them? Dawn would just die. She's really like a child. She's been so protected."

"I've thought about that myself." He looked at Sarah quickly and said, "And I've thought about what would happen if they separated us."

"Oh, that can't happen!"

"It might. Gant's no man to overlook money. He's not very smart, but he's greedy enough to make up for it. He'll be coming back soon."

A silence fell over them again, and for a while they sat just thinking. Sarah recalled how many adventures they had gone through together. She said, "I remember back in Oldworld, you didn't like me very much when I first came to stay with your family." Sarah's parents had to be overseas, and Josh's family had taken her in.

"That's what you think," Josh said. "I took one look at you and said, 'That's the prettiest girl I ever saw in my life!'"

Sarah turned to face him. "You do have your moments, Josh." Then she frowned. "You certainly kept your thoughts to yourself, though."

"Ah, well . . . I was an ugly, gawky kid. Couldn't walk without falling down. Couldn't play sports. I knew you'd be taken with the other guys."

"I wasn't though. I always liked you—from the very first. Best friends, aren't we, Josh?"

Josh reached over and took her hand. "Best friends." He smiled.

They were out of their cage and in the middle of supper when the door slammed, and Sarah looked up to see Gant come in.

His round, blunt features were flushed, and his eyes gleamed. "I'm home," he said, "and look what I have."

Reaching into his pocket, the giant pulled out a leather bag. He opened the string that held it together and poured out the contents on the table by the Sleepers' cage. "Gold," he said. "Did you ever see so much gold, wife?"

Gant's wife picked up a coin. "My," she said, "think what I can buy with this—a new dress!"

"You can have five new dresses, if you like." Gant grinned. He reached down and hugged Olina. "And you can have that pony you've been begging me for. How do you like that?"

Olina's eyes gleamed. "Where did you get it all, Papa?"

"I sold the two Little People—to the king, no less."

Gant's wife and Olina sat down while the giant boasted how he had forced the king to pay a high price for his wares. He ignored the Sleepers as though they were animals—livestock—not to be considered.

While he talked, Dave walked up to one of the coins. It was more than a foot in diameter and very thick. He struggled to pick it up but could not. "It's made out of solid gold," he said. "Think what this would be worth back home. Why, we could all live like kings on what was in this bag."

"We're not likely to get a chance," Jake grumbled. But he came over too and examined the coins with interest. "If he got this much for the captain and Dawn, he'll be wanting to get more for us," he guessed shrewdly.

Jake was not wrong. As soon as Gant had finished his story, he turned and stood over the Sleepers, grinning broadly. "These Little People—they're my gold mine," he said. "But I won't be fool enough to let the king know about them."

"What will you do?" Gant's wife asked.

"I'll take one of them at a time. Nobody knows that I have more. And I'll take them far away where some of the rich people up in the north country are. Why, they've got as much money as the king, and they'll all want to have what the king has. You know how rich people are."

"But the Little People won't like being separated!" Olina protested. She looked down at Sarah's distressed face. "See . . . look . . . they don't like it."

Gant shrugged. "They won't mind. They'll be well fed."

"But they'll be lonesome."

"Maybe they'll get 'em a pet, a bird or something else small. That would be something—pets having pets— wouldn't it?"

He stretched hugely and said, "I'll rest up tomorrow and go buy me a horse and a wagon. I'm going in style this time. But day after tomorrow, I'll pick one of them out." He leaned over and studied them all. His hand shot out, and he picked up Sarah. "This one—she talks a lot. She ought to be nice."

"No, that's my favorite!"

Gant patted Olina on the head with his free hand. "As I say, you'll have a pony. You won't miss this one. And you've got six more to play with—for a while."

"Are you going to sell them all?" Olina protested, tears in her eyes.

"Oh, I may let you keep one. You can pick any one you like."

"Then I pick that one," Olina said quickly, pointing at Sarah.

"Well, all right. She's a special pet of yours." Gant put Sarah down and snatched up Abbey. "Then I'll take this one. She'll do just as well."

There was misery among the Sleepers that night. Abbey was pale. Dave put his arm around her on one side, and Sarah did the same on the other.

"I'll never see any of you again," Abbey said. Her lips

were drawn into a tight line, and she was fighting against tears. "All of us will be alone."

"It would be a nice time for Goél to come and settle all of this." Josh had spoken impulsively, and for a moment hope gleamed in his eyes. "But he's taught us to use our heads to get out of our troubles whenever we can. I guess we should try harder. And when we really need him, we can count on him to come."

Jake's face was a mask of gloom. "We'd better try harder, because all we've got is a little while, then Abbey'll be gone—and then all of us."

"We've sure got to do something," Josh said. "We have to think of a way out of this."

Sarah squeezed his arm approvingly. "You'll think of something." She smiled faintly. "You always do, Josh Adams."

11

A Piece of String

Gant left early in the morning, his booming voice saying, "I'll be back with a horse and carriage late tonight. Tomorrow I'll leave to sell that pretty little doll of yours."

Josh looked at Abbey. She turned white and looked up at Dave, who was standing beside her. "It frightens me to think of it, Dave. Just think what it'll be like being all alone in a cage somewhere. I won't have you or any of the others to talk to."

Dave put his arm around her and drew her close. His voice was husky as he said, "Somehow I know it's going to be all right. Every jam we've gotten into looked like it was impossible to get out of at the time, but Goél always made a way."

"But all the other times we were on some kind of quest for Goél," Abbey said quietly. "This time we're just on a vacation."

Dave's handsome face was totally serious, and Josh thought he had grown up a great deal over the past months. Now his blue eyes were filled with compassion for the girl. "Somehow," he said, "I don't think Goél is interested in us only when we're doing his work. He's interested in us all the time. He likes us just for ourselves."

"Do you think that, Dave?"

"Sure I do, and he'll somehow get us out of this fix too."

Late that afternoon Olina took a nap, and the Sleepers,

having nothing to do, lay around resting. A cloud of sadness hung over the cage.

Most of them were asleep, but Abbey and Jake were restless and talked quietly. Abbey knew that Jake knew she was worried. He did not allude to the fact that she would be taken away first but told her stories about his boyhood in Oldworld, trying to make her laugh.

But Abbey could not put out of her mind the future that seemed so dark, and after a while both fell silent.

Then, "I just wish we'd never come on this trip," Jake said moodily.

"So do I," Abbey agreed. "I've complained so much about some of the things that have happened to us on our adventures, but this is absolutely the worst."

"Hey, guess what! Guess what!"

The two looked up at Wash, who had been lying on a pad made out of one of Olina's handkerchiefs. He was sitting up and scratching his head, and there was a strange look in his eye. "I just had a dream."

"A nightmare?" Jake asked.

"No, no, it was a good dream. I dreamed about Goél."

"Tell us about it!" Abbey and Jake exclaimed at once. So many times in the past when things had been absolutely bleak, Goél had come to them—either in person or in a dream but always to bring encouragement.

Wash looked at them blankly. "I can't remember. I was just asleep, you know, and I seemed to see him like he always looks. He has such a nice, kind face, but I can't remember anything else."

"What good is a dream like that?" Jake demanded. "It's important when Goél talks to us. You've *got* to remember."

"Well, I can't help it," Wash said, looking half angry at himself. Always before, the others had known exactly what Goél said. "It's right on the edge of my mind, but I just can't get hold of it."

"Maybe you'll think of it soon. Try hard. It's real important," Abbey pleaded.

"Yeah, yeah, I'll do that. I'll think *real* hard."

After Olina's nap, she took them outside. They went for a ride on the board in the pond, and a fish, almost as large as the boat, came up and stared at Wash and Abbey as they poled around.

"Did you think of it yet, Wash? What Goél said?"

"Not yet," he said, "but I'm working on it."

All afternoon Abbey tried to make the sun slow down. But it seemed to be falling rapidly, and she knew this would be her last night with her friends unless a miracle happened.

The others all seemed sober too. Their turn was coming, but she knew they all felt especially sorry for her, who would be the first to go.

Reb tried to make her laugh. There was a hen that was interested in the small people. She was much higher than Reb's head and had a sharp beak. She came by and pecked at him, and Reb slapped her on the head, then grabbed her around the neck. The hen began to cluck and flutter away, but Reb threw himself over the bird's back.

"Come on, chicken!" he said. "Let's see some good old-time Texas-style bucking!"

The Sleepers gathered around, watching as the chicken ran wildly around the yard. They were inside a small fence and could not escape, so Olina let them have their fun. Reb hollered and jerked off the Stetson that he had preserved through the shipwreck and, holding onto a handful of feathers, yelled shrilly, "Come on, let's see some bucking!"

The poor hen, however, had never had anything like this happen to her before. She flapped about in circles, clucking wildly.

Everyone was laughing, even Abbey.

Finally Reb patted the hen on the head. "You're all right, old girl," he said. "Not much of a bucker, but you'd sure make a big platter of fried chicken." He slipped to the ground and walked over to Abbey. "How about you having a ride, Abbey? I'll hold this critter down for you."

"No, thank you, Reb." She smiled. "Nice of you to offer, but I've never had much of a desire to ride a chicken."

As it grew darker, Olina put the Sleepers into their box and took them back into the house. While she helped her mother set the table, the Sleepers as usual sat at their own little table on their rough chairs.

By chance, they had fried chicken for supper. Olina took one leg and put it in the middle of the table and laughed as the Sleepers stared at it. "There's your supper. You want me to cut it up for you?"

"You'll have to," Reb shouted. "That leg's as big as an ox."

Olina took a sharp knife and cut the meat into small fragments. She also spooned out some gravy into a small bowl, and they all dipped their bread into it.

Abbey was not eating; she was glad no one said anything to her about it.

Just as they were finishing, she heard Gant's voice, and he entered, talking excitedly about the wagon and the horses he'd bought.

"I'll leave first thing in the morning," he said, squeezing his wife and mussing Olina's hair. "When I come back, I'll have enough gold to buy the best pony you ever saw."

That spoiled the evening for all of the Sleepers, and everyone seemed glad when Olina put them into their cage. The door was always firmly fastened at the top with a latch that none of them could reach. They had tried every way they could think of but had found no way to get at it.

Finally the giants were in bed, and silence fell over the house. It was then that Abbey began to cry. She made no noise about it for a while, then finally could not contain a sob.

At that Sarah reached over and pulled her close. "Don't cry," she said. "Please don't cry."

"I can't help it! I can't stand the thought of being all alone!"

"It scares me too. The rest of us will go the same way if Gant has his way."

Then the Sleepers all gathered on the girls' side of the partition, drawn together by their mutual peril. They stood and talked softly for a long time—all except Wash, who sat with his back to the side of the cage, his head bowed. He was obviously thinking hard.

Josh tried to encourage them all. Then he said, "I'm sorry—I'm not much of a leader to get us into a thing like this."

"Why, it's not your fault, Josh," Sarah said. "We all wanted to come."

"Yes, and nobody could have known how a thing like this would wind up," Dave added. "Besides, it's not over yet."

Jake shook his head stubbornly. He was pessimistic by nature and said, "Well, it's almost over. I hate to see that morning sun—"

"*I got it!*"

Abbey and everyone else turned and looked at Wash, who was scrambling to stand up. "I'm a pretty slow thinker, but I just finally remembered what it was that Goél said to me."

"What was it?" they all cried, their eyes fixed on the boy's dark face.

113

"Well, it just all come rushing back while I was sitting here," he said slowly. His eyes glowed, and he smiled. "He told me that he hadn't forgotten about us. Said that he knew all about our trip here, all about the shipwreck. I guess he knows everything." Wash shook his head in admiration. "I dreamed I asked him, 'But Goél, how're we going to get out of here?'"

"And what did he say?" Jake demanded.

"He said, 'All you need is to do a little more fishing.'"

Silence ran around the group. The Sleepers looked at each other, then their eyes came back to Wash.

"What does *that* mean?" Jake said. "We need to do a little more fishing?"

"Well, I don't know about that, but that's what he said in my dream."

"That's no good," Jake said. He flung himself down and struck the side of the cage with his fist. "You just ate too much of something."

"I don't think so," Josh said slowly. He seemed to be thinking hard. "Goél has always come like this, sometimes in person but sometimes in a dream. The first time he came to me, we were in a jail. I didn't know him very well, but he came, and I saw him, but nobody else could. I think this is like that."

"I think so too," Sarah said quickly. "Somehow, he's trying to tell us something."

"Well, I wish he'd just come out and tell us instead of hinting around." Jake grunted. "It's too scary around here to fool around with guessing."

"I think he likes us to figure out things for ourselves," Sarah said slowly. She tapped her chin thoughtfully with her forefinger. "Going fishing—going fishing—what in the world could that mean?"

"Well, it's too late to go fishing anyway. We can't go unless Olina takes us."

114

"It's too late to go to the pond or the river," Josh said, "but did he mean that?"

"What other kind of fishing is there?"

They thought hard and began to walk around the cage. Fishing. *Fishing!* It was like a game in which a riddle had to be solved.

"Goél said we had to go fishing—no, he said we had to do a little *more* fishing. What kind of fishing have we done already?" Josh was muttering out loud.

"The only fishing I know is fishing for fish," Jake said.

"Well, I've got my line here. I don't know why, but I brought it back with me," Wash said.

Abbey knew that the boys usually left their lines down by the creek. She watched Wash move over to his sleeping place and pull out the line with the hook Reb had fashioned.

"We're ready to go fishing if we just had some water." He looked around and then suddenly slapped his forehead. "We don't need no water!"

"What is it?" Abbey cried. "What do you mean, we don't need water? You have to have water for fish."

"But we ain't gonna fish for fish," Wash said. "We're gonna fish . . . for *that!*"

Wash ran up to the side of the barred cage. The slats extended far over their heads. The bottom was a board. The top was wire netting. "Right up there is the catch that holds that wire top on this old cage. They always lock it—right there. I've seen Olina do it."

"So have I," Josh said. "They put some kind of a pin in it to hold it shut. But what are you—"

"*I've* seen that!" Reb said. He looked up. "All we've got to do is climb up there, let down the line, hook that pin, and yank it out. Then we could lift the wire top off, and *then* we'd be out of this here pokey."

"That's it! That's what Goél meant!" Wash cried. "Quick! Let's see about gettin' out of here!"

The Sleepers had never tried to go up the sides of the cage before, and the climb up the bars looked too far for any of them.

"We've got to get up there and stand on that wire mesh," Wash said. "Then we can lean out through the wire and let the hook down."

"But how do we get up there?" Jake rubbed a slat and shook his head doubtfully. "It's straight up and down, and we're just not big enough."

"I know how we can do it," Abbey said. "I *knew* that being a cheerleader would come in handy someday."

"Being a cheerleader?" Josh stared at her. "What does that have to do with getting out of this place?"

"Why, we used to make a pyramid. You've seen cheerleaders do that." Her eyes were bright. "What we used to do was, three of us girls would stand together, two would get on our shoulders, then the littlest one would get up on top of those two. We could go three high that way."

"You know, I think that might work," Josh exclaimed. He looked around. "We'll put the biggest of us on the bottom and then the smaller ones as we go up." He measured the distance with his eye. "That's awfully far up—but we'll try it! It'll have to be like you said, Abbey—a pyramid."

He stood thinking hard. "OK! Here's what we'll do. Dave, you and Reb and I are about the same size. We'll form the base of the pyramid. Jake, you and Wash will get up on our shoulders. Just put your feet right there. We can hold you." He turned to the girls. "It will take two more steps on this pyramid to get to the top. Sarah, you'll have to climb up and stand on Jake and Wash."

Then he turned and said, "And Abbey, you'll have to climb all of that and then somehow get up on Sarah's

116

shoulders, and I think that'll get you up to that rim where you can do your fishing."

Abbey looked at Josh, then up to the wire-mesh top of the cage. "Well, I was always the top of the pyramid with our cheerleading group, so I guess I can do it again."

"That's the girl!" Josh grinned, giving her a quick squeeze. "All right, here we go."

Josh, Dave, and Reb faced the bars of the cage, leaning with their arms against it. Jake and Wash climbed up next. Jake put his left foot on Josh's shoulder and his right foot on Dave's. Wash did the same, except that he stood on Dave and Reb.

"All right, Sarah," Josh said, "do your stuff."

Sarah gave a jump and, pulling at the boys' clothes, managed to get to the top. "I never was much good at heights," she gasped.

"Don't look down," Josh said. "All right, Abbey, you take the line, and up you go."

Abbey looped the fishing line around her arm, putting the barbed hook through her belt. She stood behind Dave and jumped, pulling at his shoulders. When she was upright, she grasped the ankles of Jake and Wash. "I'm going to have to jump a little bit, Dave."

"Go ahead," he said. "Just step on my head. You won't hurt me there."

Sarah was atop Jake and Wash, and when Abbey finally stood just behind her—feet planted along with Sarah's on the two boys beneath—she said, "Try to support me, Sarah. I'll be as careful as I can."

"We'll be all right." Sarah's arms were out straight, pressing against the bars. "The boys are shifting," she warned. "You'd better hurry. I don't know how long we can hold you."

"All right. Here I go."

As carefully as she could, Abbey started her move. Her cheerleading acrobatics stood her in good stead. Carefully grasping Sarah's shoulders, she put one foot on Sarah's hip, then gave a lunge upward. Sarah gasped a little, but Abbey did not stop. Pulling herself up cautiously she got one foot on Sarah's shoulder, then put both her hands on her friend's head, and in one more movement stood upright.

"I'm here," she said. "I can see over."

"Be quick, Abbey," Josh gasped. "We can't stay here too much longer."

Abbey quickly unwound the fishing line and stuck her head out through the wire mesh. "I see the latch," she cried. "I'm letting down the line."

She lowered the fishing line, holding it tightly. *If I let it drop, it's all over,* she thought and grasped the string until her knuckles were white. The hook touched the pin that held the latch to the cage. It was bent in a U shape, and all she had to do was get the tip of the hook inside the U and give a yank.

That was not easy. The hook kept hitting the latch pin, but the tip of it would not go inside. Gritting her teeth, Abbey tried to be patient. She could feel the pyramid trembling beneath her. Still it would not work.

Then she felt Sarah waver. "Hold on—just a second more—"

She knew the boys at the bottom were all strong, but it sounded as if Jake and Wash were having trouble keeping their balance.

She heard Jake mutter, "I don't know if I can hold out."

"You got to!" Wash said. "You got to hold on, Jake! This is our only chance."

Abbey felt Sarah tremble even more with the unaccustomed act of balancing atop a living pyramid. Abbey knew too that her feet were grinding painfully into Sarah's shoulders. Sarah couldn't hold much longer.

Abbey took a chance. She swung the hook far out and let it swing back. Just as it hit the pin, she jerked up the line.

"I've got it!" She gave a sharp pull, and the pin came loose.

However, this was the lock that held not just the mesh top but also the side of the cage the Sleepers were leaning against. So when the latch pin was removed, that side suddenly yielded to the pressure of their weight and began to fall outward.

"Watch out!" Jake yelled. "We're falling!"

The entire side crashed, dumping all the Sleepers on the table.

Abbey had the farthest to fall. As the side of the cage hit the tabletop with a thump, she bumped her head hard, but her wrist took the hardest impact of the fall.

The Sleepers all went rolling, but there was exultation in Josh's voice as he cried, "We did it! We're out of that thing!" He ran over and helped Abbey to her feet. "Are you all right?"

"Yes, I'm all right," she said. Her head hurt, but nothing could take away from the victory they had achieved.

"Now we're getting somewhere," Reb said. "All we got to do is get out of the house."

Instantly Josh sobered. "And that's liable to be trouble. Where's that blasted cat?"

The mention of the cat sobered them all. The moon was shining through the window, and everyone looked over to the fireplace, where the cat usually slept.

There she was, her green eyes reflecting the firelight. She was watching them steadily.

"Everybody sit down and be as quiet as you can," Josh ordered. "We'll have to wait until she goes to sleep."

"Cats don't sleep very sound," Wash whispered dubiously. "We'll have to be mighty quiet."

Josh shrugged. "It's our only hope at this point."

"But how we going to get the outside door open?" Dave wanted to know. "We can't reach the knob."

"I've got an idea," Josh said, "but I'll need to think about it a little more."

"We've *got* to get out of this house," Abbey said fiercely. "We've got to."

The next hour seemed the hardest Josh had ever lived through.

The Sleepers sat absolutely motionless, scarcely breathing. Every eye was on the cat. Finally she stretched, extending her razor-sharp claws, which were as long as swords. Then she yawned, and her teeth made her look like a great white shark. At last she curled up and grew still.

None of the Sleepers stirred. For at least thirty minutes they waited. The cat did not move at all.

Josh touched Sarah's arm, put a finger to his lips, then got to his feet. He motioned for all the Sleepers to come to the far side of the tabletop. They tiptoed carefully across, and Josh pointed down to the chair that was just beneath the table.

The chair arm was only a foot or so down, and he signaled what he was going to do, framing the words silently. "Step on the chair arm—then the seat—then the rung—then the floor."

All nodded that they understood his pantomime.

Josh moved very slowly. He stepped down onto the chair arm and then onto the seat. Below the edge of the table now, he paused and looked at the cat. She still had not moved. He took a deep breath and motioned for Sarah to come ahead. The rung of the chair was just right for him to put his feet on. He carefully slid down, holding the upright leg.

Now Sarah followed, Josh helping her to the floor, and soon all seven were down.

Sarah framed the words "What are we going to do now? How do we get out?"

This was the hard time for Josh. He straightened up and pointed across the room—toward the hole where the brown rats came in from outside. He was going to lead them through the rats' tunnel!

Josh was watching Sarah. He knew what she was thinking—nothing could be worse than meeting one of those ugly creatures with their yellow teeth and bright, malicious eyes. And he well knew how dangerous it was, but he had been thinking things out. He smiled at the other Sleepers and whispered, "Come on, we can do it."

Josh approached the rat hole. The opening was very small, and there was a terrible smell as he knelt and squeezed through. Inside the tunnel it was totally dark. Josh felt his way along, expecting any moment to feel sharp teeth close on him.

And then suddenly he was outside, looking up at the stars. Drawing a sigh of relief, he helped Sarah out.

She stood up and threw her arms around him and squeezed him. Then she stepped back, and they helped the others.

They moved silently away from the house, and when they were in the bushes, Josh said, "Well, Wash, we did what Goél said, and now we've still got a long road to go."

"What are we going to do?" Reb asked.

"We're going to find Captain Daybright and Dawn, and we're going to get a ship, and we're going to get out of this awful place."

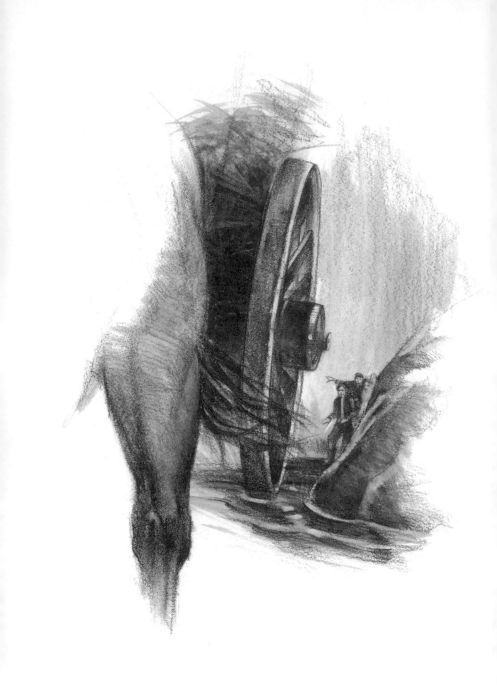

12

Dangerous Journey

The Sleepers started out at once on their dangerous journey. Through the window they had seen the direction Gant had taken Daybright and Dawn, so Josh said, "It's got to be this way. We just don't know how far."

"Gonna be dangerous traveling," Dave offered. "It'd be better to travel at night. We'd be less likely to be seen."

"Well, we can try that. Get as far as we can tonight," Josh answered. "Let's go."

They walked as rapidly as they could, staying on the edge of the road. There was no traffic at all. They passed several cottages, set well back, and from time to time they heard barking.

Abbey said nervously, "I hope those dogs don't come out here. We wouldn't have much chance."

They were startled once by a sound everyone at first thought was thunder.

Then Josh yelled, "Get off the road! It's a wagon!"

Grabbing Abbey's arm, he pulled her to one side, and the others followed. They took shelter in bushes well over their heads and stared out into the moonlight.

The horses were tall as buildings, and their hooves struck the ground so hard they seemed to rock the earth. The wagon wheels rumbled by, and the Sleepers remained where they were until the sound faded.

As they came out onto the side of the road again, Jake said shakily, "Well, at least they're not likely to sneak up on us."

They walked until dawn, then Josh said, "I think we'd better rest here—try to find something to eat."

Dave said, "Maybe I can knock down a bird." He had fashioned a leather slingshot—the kind that held a stone in a pouch while the user grasped both ends, whirling the stone around, then releasing it. Dave had gotten fairly proficient with it, and as the others started to make camp he said, "Let me go see what I can do."

"Watch out. All you need is to meet one dog, and it'd be all over," Josh warned.

"Oh, I'll be all right. We've got to have something to eat."

As they were making a small fire, Abbey said, "I wish we had stopped long enough to pack a lunch. There was plenty of food at the house."

"There was a cat too," Sarah remarked. "All I could think about was getting out of that place."

"I guess that's right," Abbey said. "Well, I'm already hungry. Let's see if we can find some berries."

They didn't find berries, but they did find a nut-bearing tree. The nuts were as big as footballs, and the shells were hard. But when Jake finally broke one open by smashing it between two rocks, he announced, "This looks good."

He broke open the rest of the shell and pulled out a kernel as big as his fist. "One of these'll do the whole bunch of us." He bit into it carefully, and his eyes opened wide. "Tastes like a pecan," he said.

They were eating the Nuworld pecan when they heard a call. "Hey! Don't spoil your appetite. Look what I got."

All looked up to see Dave coming back with something dangling over his shoulders. When he got close to them, he grinned and threw it down. "How 'bout that!"

It was a bird that looked something like a sparrow—a young bird evidently, but it was bigger than a turkey.

"Wow. How'd you ever get him, Dave?" Reb marveled.

"Just luck. I saw some of them pecking around on the ground and sneaked up on them. I let fly with a rock, and it hit this fellow right in the head. It stunned him until I could get to him." He reached down and picked up the bird with a grunt. "Bigger than any little old quail you're always bragging about, eh, Reb?"

"Why, I killed one nearly this big—me and old Blue. We was out hunting one day—"

"I don't want to hear any of your lying hunting stories," Wash said. "Let me clean that bird. We're gonna have us a feast!"

Thirty minutes later the bird was dressed, plucked, and turning on a spit over the fire.

"Mm-mm, that smells good already," Wash said. "I wish we had some black-eyed peas to go with it."

Reb nodded. "And maybe some hominy grits. That'd make it perfect."

They had none of these, but finally the bird was roasted. They plucked it apart with their bare hands.

Juggling his portion, Reb managed to get a bite and said, "This tastes near about good as a Texas quail." He bit into the bird hungrily, and soon Reb and all the Sleepers were filled to capacity.

"Never thought one little old sparrow would satisfy all seven of us," Wash said. "That's one of the best meals I ever had."

They slept as well as they could without blankets, again huddled together for warmth.

The next morning, while they ate cold sparrow for breakfast, Dave said, "You know, Josh, it could take months for us to get to wherever Daybright and Dawn are. Besides that—walking at night, did you ever stop to think what would happen if an owl sailed over?"

A silence went over the group.

Reb said, "I wouldn't want to feel one of those things sink his talons into me. They're plumb sneaky."

"Yeah, but we've *got* to go down this road," Josh argued. "I know it's dangerous, but—"

"I think we'd better try to hitch a ride, Josh—if we can," Dave said.

"Hitch a ride? How?"

"I don't know," Dave confessed, "but there'll be more wagons going down this road. If we could just get in one of them, I think we'd make it."

"Well, we'll see. I'd rather ride than walk, but if anybody sees us, we'll be goners."

Dave's suggestion lingered with Josh, and later several wagons did pass. They were moving at a high speed, however, and there was no chance to get on.

And then they came to where the road crossed a creek. There was no bridge.

Josh said, "Look at this!"

"Aw, it ain't over waist deep. We can get across it," Reb boasted.

"I don't think we want to cross it," Josh said slowly. "How about this—it's been a long, dry stretch, so what are these giant people going to do when they come to a creek?"

"I don't know what you mean, Josh," Abbey said. "What will they do?"

"Why, I think they'll stop and water their horses."

"Hey, that's just right," Reb said. "That's what we'd do back in Texas. And that gives us a chance, don't it now?"

Jake said quickly, "You mean run up and climb in the back of the wagon while the horses are drinking?"

"It might work," Josh said. "It's the best plan I've got."

As it happened, that was the way it did work. Two wagons passed by, monstrous affairs, splashing through the water without stopping.

But about midmorning Reb said, "Here comes another one. He's not moving very fast."

They all watched from their hiding place as a wagon drawn by a single lean horse and driven by an old man approached the creek.

"Whoa," the man said and stopped the horse just as its hooves were in the creek. The farmer—that seemed to be what he was—allowed the horse to drink.

The old man appeared to be half asleep, and Josh whispered, "Here's our chance. Get to the back of the wagon."

They scooted out, making as little noise as possible.

The wagon bed was at least twenty feet over their heads, but Reb said, "Quick, climb the spokes—they're as good as stairsteps!" He climbed them quickly himself and then leaned over. "This is great! There's straw in here. We can hide."

Josh helped Abbey up, then Sarah. He saw that the wagon was indeed filled with hay, on top of which were enormous melons.

When Wash was aboard, he thumped one and said, "Looks a little bit like a cantaloupe. Maybe we'll try one."

"Let's get hidden first," Josh advised. "We'll see what's going on. And see where he takes us. He might be going home."

"I bet he's going to sell these melons," Abbey said. "He'd be going to town with them then, and when we get there we can hide out and listen and find out where the palace is."

Even as she spoke, the farmer said, "Giddup!" and the horse moved forward with a jerk.

It was pleasant riding in the wagon. They kept hidden under the hay, very close to each other.

Josh said, "As soon as it stops we'll have to get out, or we'll get caught."

The trip was fairly long, and the shadows were lengthening when Reb risked a look out. He rose up carefully, his eyes on the old man, who was half asleep on the wagon seat. "There's several houses around," he reported. "There's a town up ahead, and over to one side it looks like what could be a castle."

They all raised their heads carefully for a look, and the closer they got the more Josh was convinced it was a castle.

"The road turns off," he whispered. "I believe he's going there."

The wagon lumbered up to a gate where some armed men stopped it. "I bring melons for the king's table," the old farmer muttered.

"Let him in," a burly guard said.

As the wagon rolled forward, the guard reached out, and Josh, watching from under the straw, saw a huge hand coming. The melon he was hiding under suddenly disappeared as well as another beside it, exposing Abbey. Quickly he jerked her aside, and she scrambled under the straw.

But the guards didn't notice. They were laughing, Josh saw, having stolen two juicy melons.

"This is the palace," Jake whispered. "That's what these guards mean. Now all we have to do is find Captain Daybright and Dawn."

"That may be a harder trick than it sounds like," Josh said. Then he grinned. "But at least we're here. We've got a chance."

13

A Touch of Humility

T his is the fanciest place I've ever lived in," Daybright said, "but I'd rather be in a hut back in our own country than here."

"Me too," Dawn said. She looked around the luxurious "apartment" that the king had ordered built for them. It was really an enormous dollhouse. Two of the rooms were like magnificent bedrooms with carpet and furniture made on a miniature scale out of the finest wood. There were purple hangings on the walls, windows to look out of. Everything desirable, except that the place was still a prison.

Their lives had been made miserable since they arrived at the palace. Every day their "house" was placed on a low table, and the multitude of visitors that came to the palace to wait on the king were peering at them constantly. There was not a moment's privacy all day. At night the house was put back in a room where they were cared for by a tall, thin giantess with a sour face.

It was now almost time for their prison to be put back for the night. Only two visitors remained, a fat young man with cruel eyes and a girl who simpered at his remarks.

"Why, they look like they're real, don't they?" the fat young man said.

He reached out a hand, and the girl said, "You're not supposed to touch them."

"I can do what I want. I'm the prince, aren't I?" He looked like anything but a prince. He was fat and had a pasty face.

Dawn tried to get away, but his pudgy fingers caught her, and he squeezed her so cruelly that she cried out.

Instantly Daybright threw himself at the giant hand. He had nothing for a weapon, but he sank his teeth into the flesh of the prince's huge thumb.

"Ow!"

The prince jerked his hand back, dropping Dawn, who fell to the floor. A look of rage came over his face, and he flicked Daybright with his finger, sending the captain reeling back against the wall with a thud.

"You're going to get in trouble for that!" the girl said.

And then the woman was there. "All right, My Prince, that's enough for the day," she scolded.

Then she looked down. Dawn was holding Daybright, who had been stunned by the impact. The woman leaned over and studied them carefully. "You're all right," she said.

When they were back in the apartment, the woman put out food and water for them, then sat down in a chair and began to read.

Dawn knew that their voices could not reach her. She said, "Are you all right, Ryland?"

Daybright shook his head. "I guess so." He grinned at her as he sat up. "I didn't do as well with that fat boy as I did with the snake."

"He's awful! They're all awful," she said. She touched his forehead tenderly. "You're going to have a bruise," she whispered.

"Well, I've had them before." He got to his feet. "Let's have something to eat. One thing about this place, we get good food."

They sat down and began to eat. The dishes were made of solid gold. And tiny knives and forks had been fashioned especially for them.

"When we get away, I wish we could take all this silverware and the plates with us," Daybright said. He took a bite and chewed thoughtfully. "Enough gold around here to buy the whole world, it seems like. At least enough to buy a ship!"

After they finished eating they sat on the couch, staring at the pictures on the walls, painted by the court painter. One was of the sea with a ship bounding through the waves.

"That fellow doesn't know how to paint ships," Daybright said. Then he added wistfully, "I'd sure like to be on the old *Dolphin* right now—a long way from here."

Dawn had nothing to say, and he asked, "What's the matter?"

"I was just thinking about the time I slapped Sarah."

"Why were you thinking about that?"

"Because when that boy hit you, he was doing exactly what I've done all my life. I've always had a horrible temper. I don't know how many servants I've hit like that."

Daybright was silent for a while, then he reached over and picked up her hand.

To her surprise, he kissed it, and she felt herself flush.

"You're not that kind of girl anymore," he said. "Whatever happens, you've come a long way to being a very sweet and generous person."

Dawn had heard compliments on her beauty all her life, but somehow this pleased her more than any of those. "I wish I could go home again," she said. "I'd like to make it up to some of the people that I was so mean to. I wouldn't treat them that way anymore."

After they had talked for a while, she said, "It's time to go to bed. I hate the thought of tomorrow—another day of being pawed and poked and laughed at."

"Let's sit up for a while. That old witch'll go to bed pretty soon, and I'll tell you some of my stories."

"Will they be true?" She smiled.

"Mostly," he said. "But in my stories, I'm always the hero, no matter what."

Before long the tall woman took the candle, put it on her bedside table, and lay down, pulling the cover over her. Soon her snores were reverberating.

"She sounds just like a sawmill," Daybright said. "But at least she can't hear us and won't tell us to be quiet. Now, about these stories. Let me tell you about the time I saved a beautiful, wealthy young woman from being devoured by an awful beast . . ."

They sat up for more than two hours. The candle burned down by the woman's bedside, and it cast a flickering yellow gleam over the room. Ryland Daybright had stopped telling his stories and was listening while Dawn told of her childhood.

At last she fell silent, and they said nothing for a time. But then Ryland raised his head alertly. "What was that?"

"I didn't hear anything."

"I did. Listen."

Dawn listened as hard as she could. Then she said, "I think I *did* hear something that time."

They got to their feet and moved to the windows. They were not real windows, of course. They would not open, but they had real glass in them.

"I can't see anything—anything different," Dawn said.

"Listen again. Did you hear that?"

This time Dawn knew she heard it. A bumping sound. Then, "Dawn! Captain!"

"It's the Sleepers!" Daybright exclaimed. "They're calling for us!" He ran to the door. It was bolted on the outside, he knew, but he beat on it and began yelling, "Here! We're in here!"

The voice came again, "All right. Be quiet—we're coming!"

Dawn joined him, her eyes large, and held onto his hand as they waited. "This is like a dream," she said. "Somebody must be playing a joke on us."

"No, that was Josh's voice," Daybright whispered.

Then the door opened, and there they were—Josh and Jake, grinning as if they had lost their minds.

"Well," Jake said, swaggering in, "here's another fine mess I've had to get you out of!"

The two rescuers were suddenly swarmed by the two captives. Captain Daybright and Dawn threw themselves onto the Sleepers and almost drove them to their knees.

Josh pulled himself loose, saying, "This is all very well, but we've got a long way to go."

Daybright put his hands on the shoulder of each boy. "I'll never forget this," he said. "I never thought either of you was particularly good-looking, but right now you're the handsomest guys I've ever seen in my life."

Dawn knew that getting out of the palace was fairly dangerous, and not until they were back into the woods could Josh tell the full story of how they had managed to find the apartment and finally set them free.

"Well," Josh said as he ended his story, "we've come this far. I guess you know what comes next."

Daybright nodded and set his jaw. "Yes, we've got to find a ship. It's the only way we have of getting away from this place."

14

Wash Makes a Find

The struggles that the Sleepers, Dawn, and Daybright endured getting back to the sea would take long to relate. They traveled mostly by night, keeping a close watch out for marauding owls. They did not manage to catch a ride on a wagon again, so it was a long journey before they finally stood on the shore and looked out over the ocean.

Ryland Daybright filled his lungs with the salt air and then expelled it, saying, "Whatever else happens, I'll never get away from the sea again!"

Josh looked out over the endless expanse of blue-green water broken by whitecaps. To him, what they had to do seemed impossible. "I don't see how we could ever find our way anywhere on the sea. It's just—nothing," he said.

"Give me a ship under my feet, Josh, and I'll show you how to find something. We have to sail east, and I know how to do that!"

"Yes, but a boat—ship—we'll never be able to build one," Dave said. "We're not shipbuilders."

The group all looked at Daybright, for he was their only hope. Josh knew that none of them, even if they had a ship, could possibly find his way across the uncharted waters.

Daybright smiled. "We've come too far together, friends, to be afraid now. We'll build a ship. Or we'll find something! I'll float across in a bathtub if I have to, but I'm going back home again!"

This salty speech cheered the rest of the group.

Josh said briskly, "Well, the first thing we'll do is build us a place to live. We've got to stay out of the reach of wild animals. And we've got to have some kind of weapons, even if it's only clubs or spears. So let's get to work on it."

Reb said, "The first thing is weapons, and I know where I can get some. That farm we passed back aways has got to have a blacksmith shop of some kind. There's bound to be old blades and things lying around that we could use. I'm going back and find something."

"I'll go with you," Dave said. "We can make bows too. And arrows."

The two boys hurried off amid warnings to be careful. The rest looked for a safe place to stay.

Dawn and Sarah went searching together.

"Look right up there!" Sarah said. "That looks like a cave."

Dawn looked up the steep, rocky bank. "It does look like an opening in the riverbank. Could we get into it?"

The cave mouth was almost hidden by a tree. Sarah discovered that by climbing the tree and out on a branch she could peer inside. "This may be just the place, Dawn. I think I could jump into it from here, but then I don't know if I could get out again. We'd better go get Captain Daybright."

Daybright came, crawled out on the limb, and leaped easily across to the ledge that was outside the cave. He disappeared into it and stayed so long that Sarah became nervous.

But then he poked his head out, saying, "This will do fine. There's a draft here. Evidently it's got a chimney kind of opening somewhere that brings the air on through.

We could even build a fire, and it would carry the smoke off."

As soon as the other boys came back, the whole thing became possible. Reb and Dave had found more than one metal instrument that could be fashioned into spearheads, and there was a small knife that could be wielded as a sword.

Daybright swished it through the air. "This will be fine. I'll trim some saplings, and we can make a ladder to get up into the cave."

The labor went on for two days. Constant raids were made on the farmstead. A dog investigated them once, but when Daybright poked at him with a spear, he yelped and went back to cower at the front of the house. At the farm they also found cloth, some smoked bacon, string, and odds and ends from the blacksmith shop. Finally on the third day they were set up in their cave.

"Well, be it ever so humble, there's no place like home," Jake said. He was leaning against the back of the cave, eating part of a huge potato that Sarah and Dawn had baked in the ashes.

It was the smallest potato they could find, yet was as big as a watermelon. It made a meal for all of them. And when they had broken it open, the steaming white meat sent forth a delicious odor.

They toasted the bacon on sticks over the fire. They even hauled to the cave an old tub that served as a storage bin for water, and a spring nearby furnished that.

"Well, this is all right," Wash said, "but I'm about ready to start building that boat."

"What about it? Could we do it, captain?" Josh demanded.

Daybright must have thought long about this. "I just don't see how," he said. "You need all kinds of special tools and forms and fittings—besides material! It's just more than we could do."

A silence fell over the cave.

Suddenly Dawn said, "We'll be all right."

Everyone looked at her, and she blushed. "I guess I've learned some hard lessons. One thing is never to give up. I'd just about given up when you came and got us out of the palace. I don't think I'll ever give up again." She looked over at Daybright, and there was a warm expression about her soft lips.

"Did you see that?" Sarah whispered to Josh.

"See what? Don't poke me in the ribs like that!"

"You are blind, Josh Adams, purely blind."

"What was I supposed to see?" Josh demanded, but Sarah merely gave him a disgusted look.

"You boys are all alike. No romance in you!"

For three more days they stayed in the cave, going out on forays for food, searching but finding nothing that could lead to the building of any kind of ship.

It was nearly dusk on the third day when Wash came running.

"I've got it—I've got it!"

Josh and the others were gathered inside the cave, feeling a little discouraged.

Daybright looked out. "You've got what?"

Wash, his eyes big, climbed the ladder and grabbed Daybright by the sleeve. "Come on, let me show you!"

The crew followed him down and then moved the ladder to its hiding place. They went through the woods, and an hour later they were still impatient. Wash had not said a word except "Come on, you've got to see this!"

"He's probably found a watermelon patch," Reb said in disgust.

Wash heard him and grinned, his white teeth flashing. "You just wait. You'll see something!"

They had just gone down into a valley when Josh heard the sound of water.

"There! Look and tell me I haven't seen nothing."

Wash pointed proudly, and Josh and the others rushed forward.

"A boat! A giant rowboat!" Josh exclaimed. "Look at it!" He waved at Wash's find, then looked around. "It must have drifted off from someplace upstream. Looks like it hasn't been used in a long time."

"Tell me I was looking for watermelons?" Wash said scornfully. "How's that, Captain Daybright?"

Daybright's eyes were alight as he scrambled aboard. It was a flat-bottomed fishing boat, big enough to carry one giant or perhaps two small ones. It was giant-size—at least thirty-five feet long and more than twelve feet wide. Two boards were firmly fastened, one in the middle and one in the rear, for seats.

"What do you think, Captain?" Wash cried. "Will it do?"

"I think it might," Daybright said.

Josh could see Daybright's fertile mind begin at once to devise ways to fit out the boat for an ocean voyage. He heard him mumbling things like "Rudder—anchors—masts," and finally he turned around and slapped Wash on the shoulder. "Wash, you're a genius. We'll fit this boat out and cross the ocean in it!"

A loud "Hooray" went up, and Josh found himself hugging all the Sleepers. He hugged Sarah a little longer than the others, whispering in her ear, "What do you think now?"

"I think Captain Daybright will get us all home. He's so big and strong and handsome."

139

Josh gave her an extra hug. "Well, you always did like us big, strong, handsome guys." He laughed when she struck at him. Then he joined in the dance on the bank, thinking about the days to come.

"There she is, ready for sea."

Daybright waved a proud hand at their ship, as he now called the fishing boat.

It looked far different than it had when Wash found it. Daybright had informed them, first off, that a flat-bottomed boat would have no chance at sea and then had produced what he called "dagger boards." These were two five-foot-long pieces that he fastened to the sides of the boat. They extended down into the water.

"These dagger boards," he said, "will cause her to ride the waves."

He stared up at the mast, which they had made with great labor. They had hewed down a sapling, some sixty feet tall but very thin. They trimmed it off square at the bottom. Then they cut out a hole in the middle seat and built a foundation for the mast.

The captain used some rope to make a hoist and an overhanging tree limb to lift the mast. It took all the strength they had to get it in an upright position, but when it was up, Daybright said, "There. Now we can have a sail. That's all we need now. We've got to find lots of line and something to use for canvas."

So they made one more foray to the farm.

When the sail was all rigged, it was tied to a cross-piece, and it looked somewhat like a quilt since it was made from odds and ends, but it could be raised and lowered. There was even a crow's nest that could be reached by climbing the small ratlines that held the mast in place. And lines ran from front to back to take the strain off the mast so that it wouldn't snap.

"Well, Quartermaster, how're the supplies?"

Josh grinned. "All loaded and ready, Captain. Water for over a month. Plenty of dried meat, smoked meat, berries. We've baked lots of biscuits, and all in all I'd say we're ready to go."

Josh and his crew had worked hard on the supplies. There would be no stopping at a store. Storing water had been the hardest problem until they had discovered big wild gourds. These, hollowed out and plugged, made excellent containers. They had filled them all with fresh water from the creek, and now they were stored as ballast, with a deck built over the top of them.

"All right, we'll shove off in the morning at dawn."

No one slept much that night. All were excited, and at daybreak they ate their last meal on shore.

Wash had managed to bring aboard some flat rocks to make a small oven, along with a supply of wood. "We can have something hot every now and then," he said. "Maybe every other day or so."

When they were all in the ship, Daybright looked up. "Unfurl the sail," he commanded.

At once Reb and Dave ran up the ratlines to the cross-piece. They untied the sail, which fell into place. A puff of wind caught it, and the ship started out.

"Here we go in *Dolphin II!*" Daybright cried.

The wind took the craft, and he turned the wheel, steering out into the middle of the stream. The banks began to flow by, and the ship picked up speed. "She handles well," Daybright said. "You've all done a good job."

Soon the creek began to widen, and then they came into an opening in the land, and there lay the sea.

A silence fell upon the group as they realized how massive the sea was and how tiny their fragile little boat. It had seemed sturdy enough back on the creek, but now it was like a mere chip tossed on the ocean.

Daybright looked at their solemn faces. "Don't worry, lads and lasses." He pointed up. "Yonder's the sun. By night, we'll have the stars. We steer to glory. Let's have a cheer for the Seven Sleepers and the good ship *Dolphin II!*"

A cheer rose up as the small vessel dipped with the first waves of the sea. The craft rocked down and up, the winds puffed the sail, and *Dolphin II* set sail for home.

15
Long Voyage

The sun burned in the sky with a pale glow. The beams it sent down were so hot that they heated the metal fastenings on the mast. When Josh touched them, he jerked his finger back.

"Ow!"

Sarah, sitting on a box beside him, looked up. Her lips were chapped and dry, and her face was sunburned. "It *is* hot, isn't it?" she whispered.

Josh looked over at the other Sleepers, who were in various poses of recline under the canvas they had rigged up to keep off the blazing sun. All had learned, however, that the sun's reflection on the water could burn them almost as quickly as its direct rays. After two weeks of sailing, those with the fairer skin, such as Sarah, were still suffering.

Josh looked back at the stern where Captain Daybright sat out in the sun, his cap pulled over his eyes, peering ahead at the horizon. Josh shook his head. "It looks like he'd burn to a crisp, but he just turns a little more coppery."

"He's lost weight," Sarah said. "I guess we all have."

The voyage had been hard. They had sailed steadily. Daybright had been cheerful enough, saying that they had a following wind. "If we had to sail against the wind, I'd begin to worry a little. But as it is, we're right on course."

"I don't see how he knows where we are," Josh said. He looked around the endless horizon. Nothing—nothing except water, water, water.

"Well, we're going east, and he says if we go that way long enough we're bound to hit land. It doesn't matter much what land it is."

"I guess that's right." Josh touched his swollen lips tenderly and said, "Sure could stand a little bit more water." The very thought of water made him thirsty. He hesitated, then shook his head. "But it's getting pretty low, isn't it?"

"Yes, we're down to a little less than a quart a day now."

"We lose that much sweating," he said. "At least the food supply's all right."

"Yes, we won't starve. The fish makes a good change, and there's a little moisture in them."

The small craft drove on, plunging into the swells and rising again. Its regular rhythm made Josh sleepy. He sat down and stared at the sail, saying nothing.

Finally Wash came over. "About time for our water ration, isn't it?"

"I guess so."

They all brightened up then.

Josh went to the small deck they had built and pulled the cover back. There were the few precious gourds filled with water. He uncapped one, and everyone lined up with his cup. He measured it out carefully, not spilling a drop, and then poured his own and capped the gourd while Sarah held his cup.

Sarah stared down at her water, so clear and tempting. "I'd like to just drink it all up as fast as I can, but it wouldn't be enough," she said.

"No, I take mine just a little sip at a time, hold it in my mouth, and let it run around. I try to see how long I can make it last," Josh said. "Make a game out of it."

"That's a good idea. I'll try that." Sarah smiled. "Let's

each take a mouthful, and we'll see who can keep it the longest."

Their game gave them something to think about. They had no other games to play, nothing to read. Even talking was an exertion under the burning sun.

They made their cups of water last for more than an hour, and then Sarah said, "Well, that's all until tomorrow. I wish you could drink seawater. There's plenty of that!"

Dusk came at last, and Dawn came to sit by Daybright.

He had been spelled by Dave for a time and had slept, but now, as the sun sank into the water, he was back at the wheel. "How are you, Dawn?"

"I'm fine," she said cheerfully.

"A little thirsty?"

"A little, but we all are."

He smiled at her, knowing this would not have been her response at one time. He gripped the helm firmly, keeping the ship on an even keel, from time to time glancing up at the sky. The stars came out, and he began to name them off to her.

She said, "I wish I knew all the stars."

"I'll teach them to you." He pointed to a bright one right overhead. "We call that one Sirius."

She smiled suddenly. "A star named Serious? That's funny."

"Well, it's spelled S-i-r-i-u-s but pronounced serious. He's a bright one, isn't he? I like him a lot. When all the others are gone, nearly always you can find him peeping out of the clouds."

Daybright talked with Dawn for a while, and finally the night breeze came up, cooling them off. For a long time they listened to the hissing of the water as it passed by the sides of the small ship and to the sound of the wind whistling around the mast and whipping the canvas.

Then she asked, "Are we going to make it, Ryland?"

He turned to look at her. The moon was out and poured its silvery beams down over her face. "I'm going to do the best I can. If the water holds out, if we don't have a storm, if the wind holds up—a lot of ifs. I'm afraid I don't know exactly where we are," he confessed.

"You've done more to save us than anyone. We won't be lost." She spoke encouraging words for a while and was rewarded by his smile. "What will you do when we get back?"

He looked at her in surprise. "Why, get a ship—sailing is all I know to do. I'm a sailor." He suddenly had a thought and looked at her. "Maybe your new husband will hire me to take the two of you on your honeymoon."

His words must have disturbed Dawn. She turned her face away. The wind blew her hair against his cheek. It was soft, and he had an impulse to reach out and touch her, but he did not.

She walked away, not speaking again.

"Not too much water this time," Josh said as Dawn came with her cup. He poured it half full, then apologized. "I'm sorry that's all."

Dawn smiled at him, her lips cracked, and whispered, "That's all right, Josh."

She went over to Sarah, who had developed a fever. "Here, Sarah, take just a sip of this."

"No, that's yours," Sarah protested. Her burned skin was painful, and the fever had put her out of her head for a time.

"Just take a sip." Dawn watched as Sarah took a swallow, moistened her lips, and said, "That's good." Then she laid the girl back down again and went to sit alone.

Reb was in the prow, thinking about Camelot. *That was the best time of my life,* he thought, *riding those fine horses, jousting with those big knights, and me doing as good as any. I want to go back there someday.*

He thought of the bright colors, the pennants fluttering from shining lances, the beautiful hues of the women's dresses at the tournaments, and his heart went back there again. Even more than for Texas, he longed for the world of Camelot.

For a long time he sat thinking; then he lifted his eyes. Small dots flitted before them, brought on by the intense heat. The saltwater made them burn. He pulled out a salt-soaked handkerchief and tried to wipe them. That made it worse.

"This blasted salt! Can't see a thing," he muttered. Finally he used his arm and the tail of his shirt and managed to look ahead. The sun was dancing across the water, making heat waves rise, and he blinked as he saw a tiny something on the horizon.

He shook his head and stared. *Maybe it's a ship. No, it doesn't look like a ship.* He almost called to the others, then he thought, *No, if it's only a cloud or something, no sense getting their hopes up.* He knew how low morale was. *We can't last more'n a day or two like this. The drinking water's about gone. Enough for another day, and we're dying of thirst already.*

He kept his eyes glued to the skyline, but for the next twenty minutes he thought he'd lost it. Then, suddenly, he saw it again! A lump on the horizon, very small but breaking the perfect line of the water.

He stood and held onto the rail. He watched the lump grow. Then he turned around and croaked, "Land! There's land ahead!"

His broken voice stirred them all, even Sarah. Everybody staggered to his feet.

"There it is! You see it?"

Josh had better eyes than most. "I see it," he said. "It looks like a mountain."

Captain Daybright's blue eyes were burning as they looked across the distance. He had the best eyes of them all. "It's a volcano," he said quietly. "We're coming to land."

Dawn looked at him, and tears came to her eyes. She whispered, "You saved us, Ryland. You've brought us through."

16

A Husband for Dawn

They landed late that day and staggered ashore.

One of the first things they did was find a creek. They buried their faces in the fresh, cool spring water, drinking until they could hold no more. Then they just plunged in, clothes and all, splashing water on each other, yelling and screaming like children.

When Dawn threw water in Daybright's face, he scooped her up and said, "I think maybe I'll just see how far I can throw you."

"No, don't!" she cried and held to him tightly.

The captain realized suddenly that he was holding a lovely young woman—and that they were not on the island of the giants anymore. He put her down and said, "Well, I guess it's time to get down to business."

A shadow crossed Dawn's face, and she nodded. "All right, Captain Daybright," she said.

To everyone's amazement, a fisherman informed Daybright that they were on an island next to the one where Dawn's future husband was king.

The man stared at Dawn and said, "You new wife for King Fazor?" When she nodded, he grinned at her crookedly and shook his head.

The fisherman gave them instructions, and the next morning the travelers boarded their ship and sailed once again.

"It's only a half-day's sail from here," Daybright said to the Sleepers. "I'm sure that the king will be able to supply us with something to wear instead of these rags we've got on."

He looked at Dawn, seeming to expect some response, but she simply nodded.

"What's the matter with Dawn?" Josh said. "Here's she's going to be queen, and she doesn't act at all happy. Maybe she's just tired, though."

Sarah looked at him in disgust. "I declare. I've told you before. You're blind as a bat, Josh Adams!" She would say no more, but she and Abbey talked a long time about Dawn's marriage.

"I still don't see how she could marry a man she's never seen," Abbey said. "But I guess that's the way things are here."

Later Abbey found opportunity to talk to Daybright. He was sitting alone in the stern; the others were forward. She asked, "What do you think about Dawn's marriage, Captain?"

He stared at her in surprise. "What do you mean, what do I think about it?"

"I mean, she's not just a woman now. Not after what we've all gone through together. Why, I feel like a sister to her."

"Well, I feel like a brother," he blustered, "and her father's given her to my care."

"Haven't you seen how unhappy she is?"

"Well, I can't do anything about that."

Abbey stared at him, her eyebrows going up. "She's going to be miserable," she warned.

"How can she be miserable? She'll be a queen. She'll have all kinds of clothes and jewelry and honor—be able to tell people what to do."

"I don't think she's like that anymore. As a matter of fact," Abbey said firmly, "I know she's not." She looked up to the prow, where Dawn was staring out at the dark smudge that marked her new home. "She's changed a lot on this voyage. She's actually become a sweet young lady."

Daybright shifted his weight and gave a twitch to the wheel, looked up at the sail blankly, then turned to stare at Abbey. "Well, she's the one who decided to marry him."

"No woman's happy getting married to a man she doesn't know."

Daybright seemed to have no answer for that. He muttered, "I don't know anything about that. Her father and the king are paying me to deliver her to him, and that's what I'm going to do."

They arrived in port and were greeted by a shocked welcoming group. It appeared to Abbey that the natives had been expecting the arrival of their new queen, but they had not expected her to arrive in such a ramshackle ship.

Nevertheless, the leader, a tall, thin, dark man wearing little more than a loincloth, said, "I take you to king." He bowed down before Dawn. "You come with us, Queen."

A procession started with Dawn at the front along with the skinny leader. She looked to one side and the other as they moved along. The houses were nothing but mud huts, and the people that followed had to be more savage in appearance than any she'd ever seen. They wore few clothes, and their hair was treated with dried mud.

Daybright was walking to the rear of the procession with Josh, Abbey, and Sarah. He took it all in and said, "Somehow I don't think this king is going to be exactly what I've always thought of as royalty."

"It does look like poor pickings, doesn't it? Maybe he keeps all the people poor, and he has all the money," Josh suggested. "That's the way some kings are."

They arrived at a hut much bigger than the rest. It had obviously been added to several times, so that it looked like a wart with monstrous growths on it.

As the parade of people approached, a man came out of the hut, and all the attendants with the arriving party began to cry, "Hail, King! Hail, King Fazor!"

Dawn stopped abruptly and looked at the king. Her heart seemed to sicken within her.

For Fazor was a thin man of some sixty years. He wore a piece of leather around his loins, and his legs and arms were skinny as sticks. He had lost most of his teeth, and his lips appeared to be stained with the dried juice of some kind of tobacco.

"Ha!" he said. "My new wife!" He came forward and pinched Dawn's arm. "I give your father much gold for you. You work hard. Make it up!" Then he turned to an attendant. "Pay the ship captain what was promised to bring my wife."

Abbey couldn't take her eyes off the king. He had protruding eyes and looked like a skinny bird as he hopped around, standing sometimes on one leg, hooking the other foot behind his knee. He had a shrill cry, birdlike also, and he began to harangue his attendants, telling them to begin the feast.

"We have many monkey cooked for you. Bridal feast! You become wife tonight."

"How awful," Abbey whispered to Sarah. "I never dreamed of such a thing."

"Neither did Dawn—look at her face," Sarah whispered back.

All the other Sleepers looked astounded as well. They

had seen some kings in their travels, but nothing like King Fazor!

"He looks like a monkey his own self," Reb said. "She can't marry a thing like that!"

Fazor continued hopping about, giving instructions, and soon the smell of burning meat began to fill the air.

Dawn was shoved into a sitting position along with a group of other women, some of them no more than twelve or thirteen, some of them old hags without a tooth in their heads.

"Who—who are these women?" Dawn asked the king.

Fazor pulled himself up to his full height, which was not much more than five feet. "Wives—King Fazor's wives," he said. "They be seventeen. He strutted about, clucking like a chicken, naming off their names. "This," he finally said, touching the oldest woman, "number one wife."

Number one wife was very old indeed, with white hair and small piggish eyes. She was also very fat. And there was a mean look about her as she stared at the newest addition to King Fazor's harem.

"You wait on number one wife." Fazor nodded, grinning with his broken teeth. "You cook her food, make things nice for her and for King Fazor."

"There's a life for you," Jake murmured to Wash.

Wash looked at Dawn's pale face and said, "That girl's done got herself in one big mess. I bet she wishes she was back home with her daddy again."

Then the celebrating began, which seemed to mean that all the natives would get as drunk as possible on some kind of palm wine that was served. Daybright took one sip and spit it out. "I wouldn't try this if I were you. It'll take the top of your head off."

Finally the time came for the high point of the festivities. The natives had eaten all the monkey that had been served, had drunk all the wine, and now could barely stand. They were singing drunkenly when King Fazor rose up and said, "Now, I marry new wife."

He walked toward Dawn, blinking his protruding eyes, and reached out to seize her arm.

Dawn jumped to her feet and away from him, her face white. Her green eyes were bright, and her red hair caught the light of the late afternoon sun. "Nothing was said to me about seventeen wives. I wouldn't marry you if you were the last man on the face of the earth!"

She turned from the astonished chieftain and walked up to Captain Daybright. She put her hand in his. "Ryland, take me home."

Abbey was close enough to hear her soft voice, and she waited breathlessly—as did the chief, who stared drunkenly at the pair.

Ryland Daybright looked at the lovely girl in front of him. Then he touched her cheek and smiled. "All right, Dawn. I'll take you home." He turned, taking her arm, and headed for the shore.

Abbey—and all the Sleepers—waited openmouthed. What would Fazor do?

But King Fazor and his men were too overcome with wine to do anything.

Reb let out a Rebel yell. "Ooowee! We're gonna leave this place!"

When they got to the ocean, Daybright said, "You'll be safe here for the night—those natives won't be in shape to do any damage until sometime tomorrow. I've got a little trading to do, thinking of the long voyage ahead—but I'll be back first thing in the morning."

Dawn touched his arm. "Where are you going, Ryland?"

"I have a surprise for all of you." That was all he

154

would say about his plans, but he added, "Don't forget—I promised. I'll take you home, Dawn."

Then he turned and left in their makeshift boat. The sail caught the breeze, and he headed in the direction of the island where they had first landed.

"What's he going to do?" Reb asked, a puzzled look in his eyes.

"I don't know," Wash said, "but he said he'd be back with a surprise. I guess we just stay here and wait until he comes."

Time seemed to crawl, and by dawn the Sleepers were all nervous, wondering when King Fazor's men would come out of the bushes.

Staring out to sea, Sarah said, "I wish the captain would come back."

And then ten minutes later—as if in response to her words—she saw something white on the horizon. "It's a ship!" she cried out. Running down to the water, she shaded her eyes, and soon the tiny white spot became a sail.

"Wow! Look at that ship!" Wash breathed behind her. "It's a honey, ain't it now!"

Then as the beautiful schooner drew close, Dawn cried out, "It's Ryland!"

Josh yelled, "It's the captain, all right! Now where did he get a ship like *that?*"

They all watched as the ship's crew smartly brought the vessel into the harbor, and when the captain jumped down, grinning broadly, he was swamped by Sleepers, pouring questions on him.

"You must have stolen that ship, Captain," Jake said. "You didn't have money to buy her!"

"That's what you think!" Ryland waved a hand at the

155

vessel, saying proudly, "All paid for—every sail and spar. And crew."

"But Ryland," Dawn asked, her eyes wide, "where did you get the money?"

Captain Daybright reached into his pocket and brought out a small brown leather bag. Opening the drawstring, he dropped three huge diamonds into his palm. "Payment for delivering the bride—we carried out our part of the bargain even though Dawn decided not to stay. I heard this ship was up for sale when we docked at the other island. It took one diamond to buy her. The rest will pay off my creditors—and you Sleepers for your fine service."

"She's so beautiful!" Dawn sighed. "What will you name her?"

Captain Daybright looked down at her. He said quietly, "I've already named her." He looked toward the ship and then back at her. "This is my ship *Dawn*," he said, and she flushed with pleasure. "A beautiful ship—named after a beautiful lady!"

17
Red Sails in the Sunset

Reb and Wash sat on the fantail of the *Dawn*. The ship cut through the water as fast as a sailfish. Overhead her white sails puffed, and there was a feeling of safety and security, which the young men both enjoyed.

"Been a nice voyage, hasn't it, Wash?" Reb said. "Nice to have a crew to do all the work. All we do is fish and eat. I could get used to that."

"Me too," Wash said. "I expect it'll be over tomorrow, though. At least that's what the captain said."

They sat listening to the hissing of the waves as the ship cleaved the waters, the sail like a white wing. Reb began to talk of Camelot. He had thought of that place a lot lately and finally said, "I'd like to go back there sometime."

Dave came up to join them. He listened as Reb talked of his dream of returning to Camelot and then said quietly, "I'd like to go back to Oldworld, but I don't guess I'll ever do that."

"No," Wash said slowly, "and you might not like it if you did."

"What do you mean by that?" Dave asked in surprise.

"I mean I heard of a book one time called *You Can't Go Home Again*. I never read it, but a fellow told me it was about a young man who grew up. He tried to go back to his hometown, and he found things just weren't the same."

"Well, I'd like to go back to mine," Dave said. "My old life, that is."

"I don't know about that," Reb said. "You're older now, Dave. I can remember lots of stuff I thought was real important when I was just a kid. It don't seem too important now." He thought of Camelot again. "Most of the time when we go back, things seem smaller and not as much fun as they were in our minds. That's why memories are pretty good, I reckon."

The two other boys stared at him, and Wash said, "I guess you're getting to be a philosopher, Reb."

At that moment, Daybright stepped up. "We're having a formal dinner tonight. I'll expect every one of you to come looking your best. Better cut each other's hair, it looks to me."

"What about yours?"

"Me too. This'll be our last meal on board all together. I want it to be a good one."

The boys had a fine time washing up and cutting each other's hair, and finally they put on such clothes as they could find. There had been some on board the ship, and they pieced together what they could.

The girls appeared at the main cabin all wearing dresses they had just about worn out. They had been pieced together and sewn and patched. Their hair, however, had been carefully done. They had clearly spent much time on that, and Josh thought they looked very pretty.

He said so at once, bowing. "My, you ladies look like you're ready for a ball. You sure look nice."

"Thank you, Josh," Sarah said. Her eyes gleamed, and her black hair was carefully done in a coronet around her head. Her eyes looked very large, and with her hair arranged this way, she looked more grown-up.

"Everyone sit down!" Captain Daybright announced. "It's time for the banquet."

This time the meal was served by some of the crew that Daybright had engaged for the voyage. It was a delicious dinner of fish, beef, stew, even fruit that had been carefully stored.

After dinner, Josh said, "I guess it's time for the speeches now, Captain. Let's have it."

Captain Daybright rose. "I've sailed with many crews," he began, "but none as fine as this one . . ." He spoke in glowing terms of the Sleepers, how courageous they were, how true to one another, and finally he reached down and picked up his glass. "I propose a toast—to Goél, who took care of us even though we never saw his face."

The toast was drunk, and then Daybright looked down the table at Dawn, who, thus far, had said scarcely a word. She had kept to herself on the voyage, and the Sleepers thought she was humiliated by her nearly disastrous marriage to the king.

Now Daybright lifted his glass again and said, "And now I propose a toast to the bride!"

"What does he mean by that?" Josh whispered. "She's not a bride. She dumped the king."

Sarah kicked him under the table. "Will you hush and listen! Maybe you'll learn something."

"To the bride," Daybright said, and they all stood.

Then Dawn Catalina rose to her feet. She had lost weight and was slender, but there was true regal beauty in her as she held her glass high. A smile came to her lips, and she said, "Now, I offer a toast to my husband-to-be, Captain Ryland Daybright."

Silence ran around the table, and then a cheer broke out.

Captain Daybright blushed scarlet even beneath his sunburn, and Dawn said loudly, "I'm getting a much better husband than I thought I would." She left her place, came around the table, and held up her arms.

Daybright put his around her and looked down, saying fondly, "And I've got a fine bride, gentle and sweet."

There was a celebration then, never to be forgotten.

Late that night after the party had broken up, once again Josh and Sarah were on deck.

They had been quiet for a long time, and then Josh said, "I guess I see what you meant, Sarah."

"About what?"

He turned to look at her. Her face was outlined in silver by the light of the moon. The breeze blew her hair, and she looked very pretty.

"You knew all about it, didn't you? About Dawn and Captain Daybright?"

"I knew she was in love with him. All you had to do was look at her. There's just something about a woman in love."

Josh stared at her for a long time. The breeze blew softly, and the moon beamed down. She seemed very young and vulnerable. Awkwardly he swallowed and, feeling a little ridiculous, said, "Well . . ."

He could say no more. He reached out and drew her to him. He kissed her and then stepped back, feeling guilty.

Sarah stared at him. "You did a sorry job of that," she said. "If you're going to kiss a girl, then do it right!"

Josh blinked. "Well, shoot! I haven't had much practice." A smile came to his lips. "Let me try that again. I believe I can get the hang of it."

The ship dipped slightly and glided on toward the mainland. A cloud covered the moon. The two stood at the rail, and Josh's arm was around her waist.

His voice came out slightly husky. "Well, Sarah," he said, "I guess we're growing up. And it looks like the Seven Sleepers are safe for a time."